"Don't you think you should be in bed?"
Cally asked softly.

Steve didn't argue, although the shower had made him feel better. Padding over to the bed he got in, then pulled out the towel he'd had wrapped around him. "I never wear anything in bed anyway," he said.

"I see." Cally kept her eyes on the food tray, anywhere but on Steve's body, only partly concealed by the sheet. "You should be careful about your wet hair," she added quickly.

"Want to dry it for me?" he asked.

"No." Touching him was the last thing she intended to do.

Steve devoured the homemade soup she'd placed before him. "You're a marvelous cook. The soup was delicious."

"You need your strength," she replied.

"Who needs strength to lie around in bed?" His mouth curved into a smile, the most deadly, dangerous, inviting smile she'd ever seen. It didn't help to remember it was the only thing he was wearing. . . .

WHAT ARE *LOVESWEPT* ROMANCES?

They are stories of true romance and touching emotion. We believe those two very important ingredients are constants in our highly sensual and very believable stories in the *LOVESWEPT* line. Our goal is to give you, the reader, stories of consistently high quality that may sometimes make you laugh, sometimes make you cry, but are always fresh and creative and contain many delightful surprises within their pages.

Most romance fans read an enormous number of books. Those they truly love, they keep. Others may be traded with friends and soon forgotten. We hope that each *LOVESWEPT* romance will be a treasure—a "keeper." We will always try to publish

LOVE STORIES YOU'LL NEVER FORGET
BY AUTHORS YOU'LL ALWAYS REMEMBER

The Editors

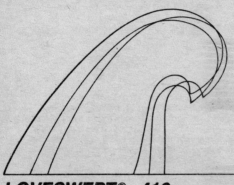

LOVESWEPT® • 416

Terry Lawrence
Wanted:
The Perfect Man

 BANTAM BOOKS
NEW YORK • TORONTO • LONDON • SYDNEY • AUCKLAND

WANTED: THE PERFECT MAN

A Bantam Book / August 1990

*LOVESWEPT® and the wave device are registered
trademarks of Bantam Books, a division of
Bantam Doubleday Dell Publishing Group, Inc.
Registered in U.S. Patent
and Trademark Office and elsewhere.*

ISBN 0-553-44046-2

Published simultaneously in the United States and Canada

---

*Bantam Books are published by Bantam Books, a division
of Bantam Doubleday Dell Publishing Group, Inc. Its trademark, consisting of the words "Bantam Books" and the
portrayal of a rooster, is Registered in U.S. Patent and
Trademark Office and in other countries. Marca Registrada. Bantam Books, 666 Fifth Avenue, New York, New
York 10103*

PRINTED IN THE UNITED STATES OF AMERICA

OPM   0 9 8 7 6 5 4 3 2 1

One

"Marlin, you're history, and I was always bored by history. I suggest you go and don't come back."

Marlin smiled a sickly smile but made no move to leave the bar.

Cally hated doing this so publicly, but she wanted it over with. Fast. "I got a call from your wife. Get the picture?"

Marlin tightened his tie. It could have been a noose considering how comfortable he appeared wearing it. "Wife? Aha. Cally, darling . . ."

"Louise? Remember her? Well, forget me. Forget my number and my name. Okay?"

Cally waited until he'd backed safely out of the bar, peering at the potted palms as if he expected his wife to jump out from behind any one of them. She sat down heavily on the stool. Her head was swimming, her hands were clammy, but she'd be damned if she'd let them shake. She wasn't about to burst into tears, not here. She'd made some major mistakes in her love life, but never had she gotten involved with a married man.

She swung around to face the bar, her knees bumping the man beside her. "Excuse me."

"Anytime." He smiled.

This one was handsome, darned handsome.

And the last thing Cally needed. A married man! How could she? She hadn't known, but couldn't she have at least suspected? Weren't there always clues?

"Would you like a drink?" the man beside her asked.

She wasn't in the mood for advances, but he'd gotten the bartender's attention. All Cally wanted was to quiet her nerves and soothe a pounding headache.

"Wine?" her self-anointed escort asked.

"Bourbon," she replied.

"I'll have what the lady's having. By the way"— he swiveled in her direction, the fabric of his slacks just brushing the silk stockings covering her knees—"my name's Steve Rousseau."

"Nice to meet you," Cally replied, staring at the wood grain of the bar. "Would you mind if we just sat here a moment? I'm not in the mood for small talk."

"I understand."

The worst part was, he sounded as if he did.

Cally's drink arrived. She gulped it, choked, blinked, and gulped some more. It certainly cleared her head. Like liquid dynamite.

Rotating her shoulders, she worked the knot of tension out of her neck. The black chiffon caressed the bare skin of her back, making whispery sounds.

She circled the half-empty glass in the puddle of moisture on the bar, waiting for the fireworks in her stomach to die down.

"You like bourbon?"

"Only when it's medicinal," she replied. "This, my friend, is long needed." To clear her head, and her heart as well. Cally grew cold inside every time she remembered the phone call.

Hello, Miss Baldwin? You don't know me, but my name's Louise Kinross, Mrs. Marlin Kinross, and I'd like you to stop seeing my husband.

"You certainly know how to pick them," Cally muttered under her breath. It was practically her motto, repeated regularly among her friends every time Cally wailed about the latest cheat, incipient alcoholic, or loser invading her life.

She had to stop. No more men! She finished her drink and banged the glass down. Except for the buzzing in her ears, she felt exhilarated, really onto something. If she could exclude men from her life, maybe she could get a handle on why she always picked the wrong ones. Deep self-examination was new to her, but it had to be an improvement over ricocheting from relationship to relationship.

In the mirror behind the bar she watched Steve glance her way in concern. The glass in front of her was empty. And for the first time that day, she felt ready to eat something.

Unfortunately, the trendy restaurant drew yuppies like bees to honey. There was a line out onto the street for those who weren't lucky enough to have a seat in the bar.

She swung around and tried to gauge the wait. A knee caught hers as she spun; she was suddenly face-to-face with Steve Rousseau.

"Hello, again," he said.

"Hi."

He wasn't entirely objectionable. Far from it. His black hair, long enough to be rebellious, was smoothed back sufficiently for any corporate setting. His fine suit emphasized fine shoulders. He was lean with a thin, rugged face. He was the kind of man you'd expect to see sculling at dawn, shoulders working, muscles slick over a rippled torso—in other words, the kind of man any sane woman would salivate over.

Cally felt sick to her stomach. She needed food, not company. The bourbon that had gone down so fast wanted to come right back up. She'd been reevaluating her life for fourteen hours at least; she hadn't slept since she'd received Louise Kinross's phone call. And she'd had precisely one doughnut for breakfast and one bag of barbecued chips for lunch. She was no longer sure if the shakes were from the bourbon, the scene with Marlin, or lack of nutrition.

She addressed the maître d'. "Max, when can I get in to eat?"

Max traced a burly finger down a list of names. "Forty-five minutes."

"And my table?" the man beside her asked.

"They're clearing it now."

Steve Rousseau looked at her as if that were all she needed to hear. "Any more questions?"

Cally wasn't too impressed with his assumption that she'd meekly accept his offer. "I have a question," she replied, enunciating carefully. It was a simple question, quite reasonable, a question she'd been wanting to ask a man for years. "Do I look like flypaper trying to catch flies?"

There was a spark of surprise in his eyes, but he kept smiling.

"Why do I always attract the wrong men? Is it something I said?"

"Uh, I don't know."

"I'm glad you think it's funny."

"I think you could use some food."

"We agree on that at least."

"I don't usually horn in on single ladies—"

"You like married ones?"

"I meant 'single' as in unaccompanied."

"Because I just got rid of a married one. That is absolutely against my rules."

"Mine too. So is taking advantage of tipsy women."

"I'm not tipsy. I'm upset. I've had a very bad day, and night, and I just dumped the most recent mistake of my mistake-strewn love life. If I were flypaper, he'd be lord of the flies."

"Yes, well. About dinner?" He was off his stool and indicating the way to the dining room.

It suddenly became very important that Cally discuss her problem with someone. A stranger, especially a reasonable, patient male one, seemed an eminently sensible sounding board. "I want a man who's honest and isn't threatened by an intelligent, beautiful woman. Is that too much to ask?"

"It might be more than some men could handle," he replied. His gaze rode slowly down her body. Obviously he agreed with her on the beautiful part. And just as obviously, he didn't include himself with the men who couldn't handle it.

Cally knew she had on nothing more scintillating than a simple black chiffon dress. As she perched on a stool with her legs crossed, her skirt rose just above her knee. Black silk hose delineated the length of a well-shaped calf. There was no reason why her heart should flip-flop because this man clearly appreciated it.

"I don't usually drink," she said.

"I guessed that much."

He patiently picked peanuts out of the palm of

his hand, one by one, biting them in half with white, even teeth. Cally had to make a decision. Decisions, even minor ones like dinner, shouldn't be based on the way a man licked salt off the corner of his mouth, or smiled at her in that beguiling way.

Feeling as if a roller coaster were suddenly taking a plunge from her heart to somewhere in her solar plexus, she swayed. "Sorry, Steve, but I need air more than food." What she needed was a shrink! She would not be attracted to another man. This was precisely the roller coaster she'd told herself she wanted off not five minutes before.

As she stepped off the stool his hand found the small of her back, steadying her.

"Careful," he said.

"My thoughts exactly," Cally murmured.

"I do think you should have something to eat before you head outside."

"Tell me, Steve, do you usually pick up drunk women?"

"Only if they fall," he said with a laugh.

How did he know her high heels were becoming treacherous and unreliable? His hand was at her lower back again. Alert. Possessive. Attentive as a lover's. Of course, good looks were hardly the measure of good intentions—as Cally had learned from Brad, or had it been Josh? "Just don't get any ideas about taking advantage of me!"

Steve grinned and ducked his head, glancing around the bar. "Would you mind saying that a little louder? I think some people in the farthest corners didn't hear it."

"If you think just because I don't usually drink—uh—"

As she tried to remember what it was she was going to accuse him of thinking, he escorted her through a crowded labyrinth of tables and chairs, each one a looming obstacle. Since when did they make restaurants so tricky to navigate? Cally wondered.

Max was pulling out her chair. Maybe it'd be a good idea to plop down before she fell down.

"Thanks, Max," Steve said. "Perhaps we could begin with some bread."

"I'll stay for one drink and that's it," Cally announced. "Then I'm taking a taxi home. Alone." Somehow she had a menu in her hands. She would read it once the letters stopped moving around.

"Where do you work, Cally?"

He was passing her a basket of fresh-baked garlic bread. The aroma was enough to give her an appetite. She tore off a piece. "The *Journal for Policy Issues in Political Science.* Near Columbia University."

"Sounds like a CIA front."

"It's a think tank."

"Same difference."

The waiter reappeared. "Would you care for wine with your dinner?"

Cally could feel herself turning green and stared hard at the plain white linen tablecloth and heavy white dishes.

"No, thank you," Steve replied for them. "Hope you like your steak rare."

"Pardon?" Her ears were ringing again. She blinked when she noticed the menus were gone.

"I ordered for us. Whatever they could bring fastest."

The bread helped. The room stopped tilting

long enough for her to get a better look at the man across from her. "Since when do you wear glasses?"

"Since they brought the menus. Required for reading."

The menus were gone, and he made no move to take the glasses off. At least he wasn't vain. Or maybe he was, Cally speculated. They were great glasses. They also made him look five years younger. "How old are you?" It was such a blunt question, Steve wasn't the only one who was surprised by it. "Uh, I mean—"

"Thirty-nine."

"Oh." At least it was a number. Concrete. Something to hold on to. She began to really focus on him. "You don't look it."

"Thank you, Cally."

"I don't remember introducing myself."

"Your friend back in the bar called you—"

"Oh. Baldwin."

He frowned. "Is that his name?"

"No, mine. Cally Baldwin. That was Marlin. He's a louse. Sorry you had to see that. I've never been accused of being shy, but I don't usually make scenes."

"I won't pry, but I'm glad you got rid of the snake. No sense his slithering through the Caesar salad."

"Say that three times fast."

"Slithering through the Thesar Thal—Ha. Can you?"

"I couldn't even say the alphabet right now."

"Feeling better?"

She gazed into blue eyes and at the flicker of candlelight on his wire-rim glasses. She wished he'd take them off. She liked the way they made him look. Smart but sensitive. She fought off that familiar, hopeful feeling.

No way. She wasn't in the market. Not even for gorgeous and pseudosensitive. She didn't have to be "on." She was free to be herself for a change. As if dipping a toe in cold water, she tried a whole new approach.

"Well, Steve, I'm flattered by all this attention. But to tell you the truth, I'm not interested in men. Not at the moment. You've heard of the New Celibacy?"

He almost choked on his water, buying a few seconds, then making innocuous remarks until the steaks arrived.

Cally was sticking to her guns. This wasn't a date. "I'll be paying my own way, thank you just the same."

"Never." He tossed his napkin down like a gauntlet. "I always pay. It's old-fashioned and no doubt chauvinistic, but that's it."

She had no intention of bristling until he made that cutting motion with his hand signifying no further discussion. "Is this a power thing?"

"Just the opposite. I live in abject fear of my mother's transcontinental disapproval. She'd hear about it, I know it." He hunched his shoulders, shuddered, and cast a wary glance over his shoulder.

Cally laughed.

"Maybe I should bring that phobia up with my analyst," he said, dropping that little bomb into the dinner conversation.

"Analyst?" Cally asked cautiously. The last thing she needed was a rundown of someone else's neuroses. She was still discovering her own. She chewed faster.

"It's not what you think," he said.

"No?"

"I'm going in for a psychological profile. I'm up for a promotion. High-stress position. They want to be sure I can handle the hours, the responsibility, the confidentiality."

"And that you don't pick up strange women too often?"

"I'll bring that up with her too."

"She's a she?"

"Dr. Martha Curtis. Seventh Avenue."

"Mmm. Don't think she could help me." Although the idea that she needed a shrink seemed to be bobbing somewhere in her memory. "I've given up on relationships. Permanently."

Steve put down his fork. "At least dinner isn't a relationship."

"I'll remember that."

He was funny. Gallant. He liked helping women in distress. She studied him through lowered lashes; six feet tall with black hair that she bet was wavy when it was wet; blue eyes like a morning sky glimpsed from the kitchen window of her apartment.

She sliced off a chunk of steak. She wasn't interested, and that was that.

The conversation lagged, a problem Steve rarely ran into. Most women were happy to keep the talk flowing. Apparently this one wasn't. That was a change. And a challenge.

"Let me try this one on you," he said. "If you were on a desert island, which three movies would you want?" It was lame, but it was better than silence.

Cally rolled her eyes. "You're not serious."

"Humor me."

"Okay. How do I get water?"

Steve signaled the waiter.

Cally reached across the table and touched his hand. "No, I meant on my desert island. With no fresh water I'd be dead within a week."

Touching him hadn't been part of the game plan. She put her hand in her lap.

Steve grinned. "You have unlimited fresh water from a flowing waterfall," he said. "You like to stand under it in the hot part of the day washing the sand from your body."

"And food?" she interrupted, dashing the word picture and the unwarranted sensations it elicited to bits. "Sorry, but I can't get into nuts and berries." She speared another cube of steak.

"C rations. Left over from World War Two by American GI's but still in remarkably good shape."

At least the man had an imagination.

"And what about a VCR to play these movies on?"

"You've got one."

"And a TV to hook it up to?"

"And cables and electricity."

"How?"

"Solar-powered batteries!" She wasn't making it easy, but he was one step ahead of her this time.

"Ooooo-kay." Cally considered for a moment. "How about *Curse of the Cat People, Dumbo,* and *Never Give a Sucker an Even Break.*"

"Are those personal opinions or movie titles?"

She smiled subtly while Steve considered her choices. A B horror movie, a cartoon, and a W. C. Fields comedy. Was she that multifaceted or merely throwing him off the scent? "Interesting choices."

"They're all seventy mintues long. Don't want to run down my batteries."

Steve fastened a wry glance on her. Make that multifaceted and a demon with logic, not to mention movie trivia. "If you could have *any* three movies . . ."

"Sorry, I can't have any."

"Why not?"

She was into this now. She could picture the island, the waves, the sand. She could picture Steve under the waterfall with her, but she didn't want to. "I can't watch any movies because I ruined the VCR."

"Pardon me?"

"I was using the solar panels to magnify light so I could start a small fire. I got burned and dropped it. When I tried to take it apart to fix it, I found the microchips inside and decided to wear them as earrings."

"Makes perfect sense to me."

"Then these Polynesian natives in canoes came paddling by, took one look, and escorted me back to their island to become their goddess."

"Of course."

"The blue eyes do it every time."

"I'll say."

Cally deftly avoided the compliment. "A goddess's life is so full." She sighed. "What with myths, incantations, and sacrifices. I haven't had time to watch any movies. Sorry. How about you?"

"Me?" His head was spinning.

"What three movies would you . . ."

He took a deep breath. "The Russian *War and Peace, Doctor Zhivago,* and *Lawrence of Arabia.*"

"On a desert island?"

"Maybe not."

"Why those?"

"They're long."

"Is that all?"

They were also romantic, grand, and had a scope Steve liked in his fantasies. Men moved mountains and crossed deserts. History itself couldn't sweep away passion.

Cally was looking at him blandly, her head tipped to one side, brunette hair falling in waves to shoulders that were bare but for the thin sheath of chiffon. "Guess I have trouble conversing with goddesses. Let me ask another question."

"Shoot."

"What three movies would you rent for an evening at my place? The wine's on me."

"Getting me drunk again?"

"Hardly."

She almost answered him. The pretend evening was disconcertingly easy to picture, until she got to the good-night kiss. Her eyes reverted to what was left of the steak. "Sorry, test patterns is all I can think of."

"We're staying up that late?" His smile was more predatory this time.

"We're not staying up at all."

"Straight to bed, then?"

She glared at him, not sure whom to be angrier with; him for suggesting or herself for wanting. How could she dare imagine anything at all after Marlin? Or Brad or Josh or every other mistake she'd made when she let her heart do the thinking. "Thank you for dinner." Placing a twenty beside her empty plate, she rose and walked away, steadier this time.

"Cally!"

She turned. She didn't want to be entirely rude. Neither did she want her brand-new resolve to crumble. Like the dessert tray, Steve was simply too tempting.

He came up beside her, his hand lightly on her shoulder. "I won't chase you through the restaurant," he said softly but firmly, his breath warm on her ear. "But I have a damned difficult time handing a woman a twenty in a public place, even if it is her own money."

Cally flushed and saw the money still sitting on the table.

"Give me your phone number. I'll call, you can give me an address, and I'll mail it back to you."

"Steve, I had a wonderful time." She thrust out her hand to put some distance between them. "Thanks for getting some food into me. Let's just say good night."

He was true to his word, he didn't chase her through the restaurant. Waiting on the curb for a taxi, she wholly deplored the way she half-expected him to.

Two brush-offs in one evening. What a way to start the new year.

Two

"I'd like you to tell me why you're here, Mr. Rousseau."

"You know why. The company sent me." Steve gave Dr. Curtis a long look. She was a proper, matronly woman who could put anyone at ease. Right now she seemed content to let him pace her office. It was very homey, for a psychoanalyst's office. Glancing out the floor-to-ceiling windows at the buildings across the way, Steve looked down on canyons that were New York streets nineteen stories below. It was certainly a different effect from the soothing landscapes on the walls, the classic wing chairs, the sound-softening wool carpet. The ashtray.

"How long since you gave up smoking?"

Steve stopped midstride, mentally awarding her that one. "Since it interfered with my racquetball. Hard to score points while hacking and coughing."

"Do you like scoring points?"

He grimaced. He wasn't here to give her ammunition.

An hour on the running track at the club was all he needed to handle the stress his job produced, or a competitive game of cutthroat racquetball, or lapping the pool until his lungs ached and his shoulders drooped. What he didn't need, what was definitely *adding* stress to his life, was this company-ordered visit. The only relaxation he'd had in the last few days was when he'd spent time with that woman at the restaurant. Cally.

The woman was different. She hadn't cried or raged while dispensing with the sleaze who'd cheated on her and his wife. Neither had she given Steve himself much of a chance. She'd brushed him off like so much lint. The twenty-dollar bill was still in his wallet.

The doctor was waiting for his reply.

"You want to hear about my scoring?" His grin was a self-contained swagger. It said enjoy, admire, and beware. "All right. I like a challenge and I like winning. That's it. Didn't Freud say sometimes a cigar is only a cigar?"

"Yes, and I hear it quoted quite a bit. Especially when I'm onto something."

Steve Rousseau spit out a short expletive, then caught the doctor's eye and her good-natured grin. She was teasing him, and he was too uptight to notice. He shrugged and plunged his hands into his pockets. "I'm being fidgety and defensive."

"Mmm-hmm. Would you like to talk about that?"

"No. I don't want to be here at all. I don't need analysis."

"Your company insists. Why don't you take a seat and we'll get started?"

"Cally Baldwin. I had a one-o'clock appointment." Her voice was a whisper. As disguises go, the big sunglasses were ridiculous. So was the raincoat and fedora. So was being there at all.

Cally did *not* need psychoanalysis. She was perfectly normal. Upon careful consideration she'd decided the men she'd dated were the ones with problems.

She'd read all the books about foolish choices and loving too much. She'd even attended a seminar aptly titled "All Men Are Not Jerks." Not according to her little black book.

But thoughts of Steve Rousseau flitted through her mind when she least expected them. Little voices nudged her when she was half-awake. *There is someone out there for you.* There had to be. Her resolution to avoid men was crumbling, and it wasn't even mid-January.

She kept her voice carefully low. "I had an appointment with Dr. Curtis," she hissed.

Behind the curved teak desk the receptionist flipped open a book. "The doctor is with someone right now."

"I know, I'm early, I'm sorry."

"No need to apologize."

Now she was being overly apologetic. Cally sighed and took off her raincoat. Setting the hat on a shelf, she reminded herself not to forget it. She'd borrowed it from her friend Alicia. The doctor's name she'd picked up from Mr. Rousseau.

"Sometimes you have to do more than unload on friends," Alicia had advised.

"You mean dump on them. I'm sorry, Lish. I'm being a pain."

"Just go. One session couldn't hurt. If they start talking penis envy, then leave."

"You think I need counseling?"

"I think you need to find out why you keep hooking up with the wrong men."

She'd thought about it. She would never knowingly date a married man. Nor stay too long with someone like Brad, whose idea of recreation was a vial of white powder in his jacket pocket. Two years of charmers like that tended to dent a woman's confidence in her ability to choose.

"Give it one more shot," Alicia had said. "Before you renounce all men and I have to visit you in a convent."

Cally ground her teeth, glancing at the frosted glass door and considering her escape. Here she was, reading *Field and Stream* in a shrink's office. "Cally Baldwin, what have you come to?"

An article on gun dogs caught her eye: *One More Shot.*

She sighed and flipped the page.

The chair was disconcertingly comfortable. Steve made himself at home. "There's the matter of confidentiality."

"Please feel free to discuss anything within the walls of this office."

"I don't think the company would want me telling you."

"They sent you."

With a determined furrow between his brows, he came to the point. "All right, then. I'm here because my predecessor cracked up under the strain and took half a million dollars with him."

Martha Curtis raised one eyebrow.

Steve continued, eyes focused and penetrating. It was clear that what he was saying was not to leave this office.

"The shareholders don't know it yet, but they're bound to find out. The boys downtown are running around like headless chickens. Their after-the-fact solution is to make sure his replacement is so thoroughly vetted, this kind of thing will never happen again. That's why they're putting me through this . . . psychological profile." It was a better phrase than the two-syllable word he'd had in mind.

"And what do you think of that, Steve?"

"I think you get paid a hundred dollars an hour to ask questions like 'What do you think of that, Steve?' " He gave her a brilliant flashing smile.

She shuffled a paper on her desk, but only as an interlude. She was in charge, and her ways of showing it were subtle and unmistakable. For instance, she was the one asking the questions. And sitting behind the desk. "Does talking about your feelings make you uncomfortable?"

"Not any more than letting a woman be in charge for a change." Let her jot that one down, he thought with a grin. "That's chauvinist with a capital *C*."

"Is it?"

He liked her style. Unruffled. "I like women," he said. "They're subtle, emotionally attuned, in touch with their feelings. If there were a few women in the upper echelons of AmeriConGroup, I bet someone would have noticed Doug Craddock was on the edge a lot sooner."

Although Steve doubted anyone could have predicted Doug's final gesture—stealing a company plane and dumping half a million over the poorer sections of Honduras. A solution to the problems in Central America, his farewell note said. Steve swallowed a smile.

"Many men find emotions difficult. They get quiet. Or make jokes—"

He spotted the diplomas on the wall. "Do you have to be an MD to be a psychologist? How much training exactly do you have for this?"

"—or change the subject."

He should have known. The woman wouldn't be able to afford the rent on this Manhattan high rise if she wasn't top-notch in her business.

"I enjoy feelings as much as the next man," he said, crossing his legs. "Healthy, heterosexual, man-to-woman kinds of feelings." He smiled again, looking her up and down with a long, unblinking gaze.

Dr. Curtis opened a manila folder and made some notes.

Steve rated the cost of the Waterman pen. He liked to know what things cost before he bought them.

Handsome, Dr. Curtis wrote. *Smooth and businesslike. Well-fitting, expensive suit. Indicator of self-esteem? Clean shaven, accentuates rugged underline of jaw. Keen cheekbones. Quick, perceptive blue eyes. Wide, thin mouth. Easy to imagine him considering thoughtfully, frowning icily. Flirting.*

Dr. Curtis stopped writing. "Are you flirting with me, Mr. Rosseau?" Sometimes directness got results.

Steve's grin widened imperceptibly. "If you weren't wearing that wedding ring, I might be."

"Or if I was twenty years younger?" She lifted the glasses hanging from a string around her neck and put them on, immediately recognizing it as a defense mechanism. She kept them on anyway.

"Age differences don't bother me," he said. For a brief moment Cally wandered into his mind again. She'd asked his age; he hadn't got around to asking hers. Over thirty, he'd guessed. That was good. "Experience counts for a lot in my book. Which is why I'm as qualified as anyone in AmeriConGroup for this job."

"Thank you for getting us back on the subject."

"You're welcome." Steve looked around the room, then fixed his eyes on her as if he'd come to some conclusion. "So ask away. Delve. Question. Interrogate. What do you want to hear about first, my mother, my father, or the time my gerbil died?"

"To begin, I'm going to ask you to take a test, the Minnesota Multi-Phase Personality Inventory. It's pretty standard as these things go. When you're finished, you can stop back in for a few minutes with any questions you might have."

"That's it?" This might be easier than he'd thought. He'd been foolish to get so worked up.

"After the test has been interpreted, we'll schedule two or three more sessions to discuss the results."

"More sessions?" Some men's voices rose when they were angry. Steve's lowered.

Dr. Curtis made a note. *Need for control?*

"It's hardly in-depth analysis, Mr. Rousseau. We'll discuss the basics, how you handle stress, your job, your self-image, relationships with others."

"*That* will be a short session." His relationships were zilch. Ever since Tawny had walked out. The scars were healed over, but he hadn't exactly been bragging in the locker room lately.

He ran a hand through his hair and grunted

his assent. There didn't seem to be any way out of this promotion-by-expert-testimony. Stepping into the waiting area, he was handed over to a receptionist, who was waiting on a woman in movie-star sunglasses. The woman kept her face hidden behind curtains of dark brown hair.

Not able to catch more of her, Steve shot a glance at her legs. She wore a slim black skirt that ended an inch above her knees and an inch below the long matching jacket. Five foot seven and liked high heels. It meant she was no shrinking violet. The attention-grabbing sunglasses could have told him that. Meanwhile he read a host of things into the heels; a woman who stands up for herself, who looks men in the eye.

Now *he* was the one playing analyst.

"Dr. Curtis will see you now," the receptionist replied to a whispered question. "She's just finishing with a patient."

Steve straightened. He didn't like being referred to as a patient. The woman in the glasses didn't seem to notice. She put a strand of hair behind one ear. Suddenly he recognized her. Cally.

He sidled up to her. "Do you come here often?"

To a psychiatrist's office? Cally was about to turn on him with a tart reply. "Steve!"

"I see you took me up on my offer." If she was there, she must have been hurting more than she let on at the restaurant. His voice was immediately gentler. "How are you?"

"I'm late for my appointment. Excuse me."

"Whew!" He grabbed his shoulder. "That was a cold one."

"Stop kidding around."

"If you can't be lighthearted in a shrink's office, where can you. . . ?"

"I mean it." She was fighting a grin already.

"Then let me return something you forgot at the restaurant."

"My common sense?" Cally asked.

He fished out two theater tickets.

"Those aren't mine."

"Your twenty-dollar bill mated with a ten in my wallet. This is their offspring."

"Excuse my skepticism, but what show can you see in this town for fifteen dollars per ticket?"

"A friend of mine is in it. I got a deal."

Cally sighed, for his sake. Her doubts about men were the whole reason she was there. How could she explain that?

"Steve, you're sweet." It was the best she could come up with while words such as *gorgeous*, *striking*, and *adorable* collided in her head. "But I told you, I've sworn off men for the time being. If we go out, you run the risk of hearing my life's story, and I wouldn't inflict that on anyone who isn't professionally trained."

She got him to laugh. Now if only she could get him to ease out of her way and let her pass.

"So take a friend to the show. It was your twenty." He handed her the tickets, leaned a shoulder against the wall, and crossed one long leg over the other.

How could he make such a public gesture seem so . . . intimate? "Thanks." Grudgingly, she shoved the tickets in her purse.

"Second question."

"Yes?"

"May I be the friend?"

Cally sighed. She was doing a lot of that lately. "I didn't know you were so persistent."

"You don't know me yet."

No, she didn't. "You know, the only thing crazier than picking up women in bars, is picking them up in psychiatrist's offices?"

"Consider me warned. For my part, I should point out that this show has had a very short run. I promised I'd go before it closed."

"And inflict it on me?"

He chucked her under the chin. "I bet no one ever called you coy." With that, he escorted her to the doctor's door, his hand on her lower back. She slowed slightly and the pressure increased.

She turned her head. She had every intention of looking him in the eye. Taking a deep breath to tell him "thank you but no," she got a whiff of his after-shave. Smooth. Suave. A hint of the offbeat. Power and subtlety combined. *All that in an after-shave?* "I'm sorry, Steve. I really can't."

"If you and I meet there, I'll let you pay for your own taxi."

"No. I mean, yes, I would pay—"

"I'll be waiting outside the theater. The Orpheum, Second Avenue and Eighth Street."

A purposeful stride took him down the corridor. She could imagine him barreling through any opposition. The way he just had through hers. She had half a mind to call him back. Of course, when it came to men, having half a mind was her whole problem.

"Are you Cally Baldwin?" a matronly but fashionable woman asked from the doorway. "Please come in."

The smile on Steve's face faded as the receptionist led him to an empty office. A desk, a pencil, and a questionnaire greeted him. He was already paying for Doug Craddock's Central American solution. Why be in the market for a woman with problems? Was it because she wore heels, had great legs, and a biting sense of humor? Because she refused to flirt, build up his ego, or flaunt her own?

Because he liked a challenge?

Probably.

The pencil scratched across the paper as he filled in little round circles, staying scrupulously within the lines. Would he get points for neatness? Did stray marks indicate a desire for power? Did gray areas not fully erased reveal laziness? Impulsiveness? Indecisiveness? How about careful, lovingly rounded edges? Sensuality? Thoughtfulness?

Daydreams about brunettes in dark glasses floated into his thoughts. That was normal enough. Would the doctor read any of that into his circles? How about fleeting memories of his former lover?

The lead broke. He scanned the room for a sharpener and got up.

Tawny would have hated this promotion, although it was precisely the result of all those evenings he'd devoted to work after she'd left. Dedication paid off. Ironically, the promotion would keep him busier than ever. Much too busy to think about relationships, old or new.

If he passed the test.

It shouldn't be hard. Any mental problems he had revolved around a logic-minded femme fatale who'd sworn off men. If loneliness was a way of life for him, blame it on the job.

A flicker of pain shadowed his eyes as he recognized the same tired excuse. He shook it off with a wry smile. No reason why a psychological profile should make him question his whole life.

Cally tucked a strand of hair behind her ear. Pulling off the sunglasses, she tossed her head. A tissue was crushed in her fist, and she wasn't sure how it had gotten there. Then she saw the boutique box on the corner of the desk, no doubt for first-timers like her. "I don't really need to be here."

The doctor's voice was calming, reassuring. "You made an appointment. There's usually a reason."

"I know the reasons well enough. They have names like Brad and Josh and Marlin. Especially Marlin."

Dr. Curtis smiled gently. "Men can be a problem."

"You're telling me." Cally took a deep breath. The chair was still warm. She thought of Steve—not for the first time. The jolt he gave her bloodstream was nerves, that's all. "Look, I'm not crazy."

"Very few people are."

"So what keeps you in business?" Cally responded with a laugh. She rested her chin on her hand and gave the doctor a gamin grin. The doctor seemed to relax too.

"People with problems come to me when they need help sorting them out. I'm an impartial listener."

"I think I've worn out all my other listeners. That's really why I'm here. A friend talked me into it. Somebody else gave me your name."

The same somebody whose theater tickets were in her pocket.

"Was she concerned about you?"

"Alicia? You would be, too, if you saw some of the men I've gone out with." It was a joke, an offhand remark. "They're either terrible or unavailable. Any good ones don't stay long. Alicia suspects some kind of pattern."

"And what do you think?"

Cally wadded up the shredded tissue. Glancing around the homey office, she located a wastebasket. She used the excuse to stretch her legs. Before she knew it she was pacing. She stopped with an apologetic smile. "Maybe there's a problem."

Dr. Curtis laughed softly. "Then you're halfway toward solving it." She opened a manila folder.

"First off, Cally, I don't believe in a lifetime of analysis. Six sessions should be sufficient to air your feelings and see what's behind this pattern. It won't always be easy, sometimes it'll be painful. Self-knowledge often is. However, to start, I want you to describe the perfect man to me."

"Perfect man?"

"We're going to draw up a wanted poster."

"But I don't want to find a man. I want to stop looking!"

"This will help. By describing your ideal man, you list what *you* want. Too often a woman responds to any man who shows an interest, believing she can either change him or that love will let her ignore his faults. When you compare a man to your ideal, before feelings get in the way, you're being realistic. You can also screen out anyone who doesn't measure up."

"Isn't that a little judgmental?"

"Isn't it your judgment you're questioning?"

Cally met her smile. "Where do we start?"

"Anywhere you like. I'll take notes."

"Okay. Six feet tall."

"Mmm-hmm."

"Black hair and blue eyes. I love that combination."

"Go on."

"Thin. In good shape."

"Clothes? Style?"

Here she had to say something that wasn't obviously related to Steve Rousseau. "Jeans and plaid shirts, rugged. Easygoing. Faithful. Thoughtful. Funny."

"Good."

"He should be able to put up with me. Some days I want to talk everything to death. Other times I just make jokes. I wear a sign that says 'Don't get too close.' "

"And he should be able to read those signs."

"Yes. The perfect mind-reading lover. I know, I know, that's unrealistic. How about sensitive? Witty. Unthreatened."

How about a thousand things not even a Steve Rousseau could live up to? That ought to keep her safe.

The taxi lurched out of another pothole. The driver cursed in Jamaican. "Okay wid you, lady?"

"Fine. I said fine!"

Reggae music blared as they turned onto Eighth Street.

She was going to meet Steve at the theater. Their first—and last—date. She remembered the contract.

After running over the wanted poster again, Dr. Curtis had gotten to the heart of the matter. "There is one more thing I'd like to do to end our first session, Cally. I'd like us to make up an agreement, in writing, that you will stick to your resolve to see no men until our sessions are completed."

"No dates?"

"That was one of the things you told me on the phone. That you wanted to step off this merry-go-round."

"I do."

"I think that's very sensible. Until you know what's going wrong with your relationships, it's better not to start a new one. We need to concentrate on you."

The theater tickets had sat in her pocket, stiff and unbending. "Uh, except I do have a date. Friday night."

"Do you want to go?"

Cally winced. "I paid for the tickets."

The doctor pursed her lips for a moment. "In that case. However, if you are sincere about learning from your mistakes, you need to step back from time to time. You've felt this yourself."

"I know. That's the reason I came."

"Then we'll draw up an agreement along those lines. Except for tomorrow night's date, no more men."

"No relationships, no looking. Where do I sign?"

The cab lurched to a stop in front of the theater. A man on a ladder was already changing the marquee.

"Looks like I got here just in time," Cally muttered wryly.

Steve was standing in the shadow beside the box office. He smiled when he saw her.

The collar of his plaid shirt was turned up under his leather bomber jacket. Well-worn jeans hugged his legs.

Her wanted poster waved and walked toward her.

Three

"The lobby's kind of crowded," Steve said, pressing through the throng to hand her a drink.

"Surprising," Cally murmured, "considering how many people walked out during the first act."

Steve grimaced. "I know it's not the greatest—"

"How long has it been running?"

"Three weeks."

"And it's closing tonight?"

"That's why I wanted to get down here to catch it."

"I see. That must have b en some deal you got on the tickets."

He grinned. "Want your money back?"

She laughed. He had confidence galore, just like her perfect man.

The soda went down the wrong way, and she choked. Steve patted her back until the coughing subsided. His pat became a rub, his hand moving gently up and down as the fabric of her sweater caressed her silk teddy, in turn caressing her skin. The shimmying of the material called to mind pictures of his bare hand doing the same thing to her bare skin.

"Steve." She stepped away abruptly, which was not easy to do in the crowded area near the bar.

"I feel like a thoroughbred getting a rubdown before a race." It was her heart that was racing.

"Sorry. Thought I detected some tension. Here."

He closed a large hand around the back of her neck. Underneath the shoulder-length hair, her skin was warm. The muscles *were* tense.

Whose fault was that? Cally wondered.

Her lips tightly drawn together, she refused to sigh at his touch. An involuntary moan escaped her anyway. "Do that much longer, and I'll be sound asleep before the second act is over."

"You and the rest of the audience."

She giggled. "It's really bad."

"Nothing worse than an unfunny comedy."

"Or an unmusical musical."

"Or actors who can't act."

"Or writers who can't write."

"Have we trashed the scenery yet?"

"I have a feeling we will. And the lighting."

"What there is of it," Steve commented. "Although the chain saw was highlighted nicely."

"There's been a spotlight on it all night. Wasn't it Chekhov who said, 'A chain saw introduced in the first act should be used by the last act?' "

They both shuddered at the possibilities.

"I doubt he had a musical about lumberjacks in mind," Steve replied.

The lights flickered.

"Should we go back in?" Cally asked. She had to stop standing so near him. Somehow his hand had strayed to her neck again, gently kneading. Somehow, she felt as right as rain. They could have stood there for the next hour and she wouldn't have minded. His blue eyes had so many highlights—gray, gold, a fascinating outline of black echoing his dark lashes. She wanted to study him, to decide if those crinkles were sun- or smile-induced. The lights dimmed again.

Steve broke eye contact first. Taking the half-finished drink from her hand, he set it on the counter. His voice was low, his words rushed, almost as if he weren't getting enough air. "We could have dinner someplace. Beat the crowds."

He was looking at her as if her answer mattered very much. With a shudder she realized it did. If she was ever going to get her feet on the ground, she had to say no sometime, to someone. Unfortunately that someone was Steve Rousseau.

Cally looked at the exits. There were as many people heading that way as into the theater. "The rush is already on its way." Boldly, she took his arm. She had to look unaffected, if only to fool herself. "Aren't you the least bit curious about that chain saw?"

"I'm curious about you."

"I know." They were walking side by side, she didn't have to look up. Her instincts for self-preservation demanded she keep her eyes on the aisle, the velvet curtain. "Steve, I made an agreement with Dr. Curtis today. No more men."

"You told me that when we first met. The New Celibacy?"

"Shh." Her cheeks flushed, and she glanced around as they took their seats. She was determined to set the record straight. She didn't want to lead him on, or herself. "It was a wonderful coincidence running into you at Martha's office."

"You call her Martha?"

"She makes me feel very at home. But she does think I should stop seeing people until I've got my own life in order."

" 'People' meaning men."

"Some of them qualify, yes."

He bit back a smile. "Sounds very sensible."

"You agree?" Her heart sank. Or her spirits rose. She was too tense to distinguish exactly what contortions her emotions were going through. The lights began to go down.

"What do *you* think?" he asked, his voice low, his expression hard to make out in the rapidly dwindling light.

"We signed a contract," she said.

"A what?"

"We agreed, in writing, no men until my problems are solved."

"And how many years will this take?" Was he angry or calm? His voice was so low she couldn't tell.

"Six sessions. A couple months at the most."

"And you want me to disappear until then?"

"Yes," she said with a rush of air. He *was* angry. Cally had the panicky feeling she was making the worst mistake of her life. But then, she'd made nothing but mistakes where men were concerned.

The curtain parted, and a stab of light illuminated Steve's face. He turned to her. "May I at least say good-bye?"

A startled "Oh" escaped her. She laid her hand on his on the armrest. "Can it wait till this act is over?"

A commotion on the stage distracted them, but not for long.

"Don't worry," he said, the skin around his jaw tight. "I'd never walk out and leave a lady stranded."

"Your mother would find out." She smiled weakly.

"Right," he said flatly.

The show was interminable; Cally wished it had gone on another hour. Anything to give her time to memorize Steve Rousseau's profile, the combination of his after-shave and the warmed leather of his coat.

Too soon they were on the sidewalk, Steve hailing a cab. She'd have to shake hands, say thanks, but he seemed more intent on bundling her into the taxi.

"Steve, I'm sorry about the future, it's just—"

"No problem."

Then he was on the seat beside her, shutting the door. "Want to give the man your address, or would you rather I gave him mine?"

Cally's mouth dropped open. Hastily, she evaluated the situation. Ejecting him bodily was out. She supposed saying good-bye at her place would work just as well. Scooting forward, she gave the driver her address.

The cab pulled out fast, tossing her thigh to thigh against Steve. He put his arm around her shoulders to catch her. He grinned. She didn't. With a lurch they hit the same pothole she'd hit on the way there.

"I have the results of your profile, Steve."

"Am I normal, Doc?"

"So far as that can be said of anyone."

He wasn't interested. On automatic pilot, he made all the proper responses as she asked questions.

"You don't seem to be with us today, Steve."

She didn't miss a thing. He was surrounded by clever women.

"I've been having a little trouble concentrating."

"Putting in long hours?"

"No longer than usual. It isn't the job."

Dr. Curtis waited. Steve recognized the technique. He'd spent many excruciating moments at board meetings watching men explain and elaborate and generally babble their way down the tubes trying to fill up an uncomfortable silence.

But dammit, he wanted to talk. "I met this woman."

"Yes?" She was smiling. *Go ahead, Steve, talk.*

"She has this—" What, contract? Was he going to tell Dr. Curtis he was seeing one of her clients? "She doesn't want to see me."

"And you want to see her."

"I intend to."

"Do you find that a challenge?"

"You take good notes."

The doctor glanced up from his folder with a smile of acknowledgment. "And?"

"Yes, I like a challenge." He grinned his "beware" grin. Not many women would brave that look. Dr. Curtis wasn't backing down. "But it changes my approach."

"She has reasons for not wanting to see you?"

"Yes." *And they're all yours,* he almost said. He caught himself, shifting in the chair. "I agreed to abide by her rules. More or less."

No way was he giving up after one date. The number for the *Journal for Policy Issues in Political Science* hadn't been that hard to find. As it was, he'd resisted picking up the phone until he thought he'd go nuts. He'd lasted all of three days.

"It hasn't been easy. She wants to be friends." Steve had a few choice substitutes for the word *friends.* "She's had some bad experiences."

"Then her caution is understandable."

"And I'm the one taking the blame for all the jerks in her past."

"Do you resent that?"

"Isn't that the whole reason I'm here? Someone else fluffs it, and I'm the one getting scrutinized." He shrugged impatiently, dismissing that as water under the bridge. Cally was his main concern. "If she's been hurt, I don't want to compound things."

"But?"

"But what if I'm the man she needs?"

Steve looked out the window at the glass box across the street. He'd been feeling like a lovesick Romeo all week. And for what? One dinner and a theater date? Was he that lonely? Had he ever been this quick to let someone get under his skin? Maybe it *was* the challenge.

Wrapped up in all of it was a picture he hadn't been able to get out of his head—the flicker of streetlights playing over Cally's face in the backseat of the taxi as they rode back to her place.

Thinking back on it, Steve gave her credit. For most of the ride she'd recapped the play in a lively, humorous way. Somehow she'd managed to pay attention during the second act. He certainly hadn't.

He'd had his arm around her shoulders in the taxi. The tight corners the driver had taken kept pushing her closer to him. She'd ignored his double entendres. The pink in her cheeks hadn't been all due to the subfreezing temperatures.

They stopped in front of a brownstone. Through the beveled glass door he glimpsed a half dozen mailboxes on the wall. She didn't mention which apartment was hers.

"Thanks again for the evening, Steve. It was fun. In its way."

She was joking about the play. The fact that she'd asked him to withdraw from her life didn't seem to bother her. Well, it bothered him—plenty. Especially after those few occasions during the second act when he'd turned to catch her looking at him as if she were turning down a free trip to Paris.

Perhaps, because of Dr. Curtis, she felt she'd had to.

But there were things he'd had to do too.

Like hopping out of the cab, catching her between two parked cars, taking her shoulders in his hands, and kissing her until his blood pounded. Maybe he shouldn't have. He'd go to his grave glad he did.

It had started as a good-night kiss, simple enough. Her lips had been warm, parted in surprise. She'd stiffened. He'd eased up, not forcing, not frightening, not giving up. He could have parted her lips with his tongue. That he didn't proved he'd had at least one strand of self-control left.

She'd smelled so good. Hints of her subtle perfume had teased his senses all evening. He remembered the whisper of her hair against her coat collar. He'd wanted to put his mouth where his hand had been on the back of her neck. He hadn't dared.

She'd been ready to run. He hadn't been ready to let her.

Finally they both had come up for air. That was another picture he couldn't forget. Her dark red mouth, her cheeks pale but highlighted by pink circles in the brisk winter night. Hell, she could have been Snow White and he the Prince. Only with this damsel, *he* had been the one in distress.

Particularly when her hands had parted his bomber jacket and she'd reached inside. He'd felt the cold of her hands through his shirt. They'd seared his skin.

Her tongue had parted *his* lips.

Steve stopped there, aware his breath was forming circles on the glass of Dr. Curtis's window. His fists were clenched at his sides. He cleared his throat, his memory, his veins.

But some things remained:

The sound of a taxi honking.

A hurried "Good-night" as Cally had run breathlessly up the stairs, fumbling with her keys.

Steve had handed the driver a five and had waited to see which apartment light went on.

"I want to keep seeing her, Doc."

"Then you have a dilemma."

"Tell me something I don't know. Any suggestions?"

"You need to find your own answers."

Damn right. "Unfortunately, the only answer for a woman who wants no relationship is to *have* no relationship. Wait a minute." Steve sat up on the edge of his chair, plucking at the crease in his slacks with one hand, playing with the knot in his tie with the other.

"Yes?" Martha Curtis surreptitiously glanced at her watch. The hour was almost up, and they'd spent a lot of time on this. However, the way Mr. Rousseau reached conclusions would give her a clue to his management style.

"If she doesn't want a relationship, then why don't I give her exactly what she wants?"

"Stop seeing her?"

"Just the opposite, Doc. Just the opposite."

It was Steve's turn to look at his watch. He stretched across the desk to shake her hand. "You know, Doc, this therapy isn't so bad."

The door closed behind him with a soft whoosh. Dr. Curtis shook her head. If she could figure out what decision he'd just made, she could write it down.

Cally hung her head, alternating between tucking her hair behind one ear and tearing at the ratted tissue in her hands. "I have another date," she mumbled morosely. "It's strictly a business affair. He has this company function coming up and wants a beautiful woman on his arm."

"Is that the way *he* put it?"

Unfortunately, that was exactly the way he'd put it. Cally stared at the windows but stayed rooted to the chair.

"I detect some uneasiness."

"I thought you'd be angry. Because of the contract."

"This is up to you, Cally. You make your own choices."

"And they're so often wrong." She laughed. It didn't erase the worried look in her eyes.

It had taken three phone calls for Steve to convince her he was a perfectly safe date. The subject of The Kiss never came up. They laughed about that horrible musical, discussed their work, even talked about Dr. Curtis, all without ever mentioning kisses *or* good-nights.

When it came to classic denial, Cally was an expert. She'd barely admitted to herself that she'd been the one prolonging their kiss. Nor that she'd twined her arms around his back, burrowed into the heat and warmth of his coat, wished hers had been open so she could have pressed against him, melted into his arms.

But the taxi had honked.

And the ink was barely dry on her agreement with Martha Curtis.

"It's this psychoanalysis thing," Steve had said on the phone. "I'm under a microscope at Ameri-Con. I don't mind attending these functions alone, but . . ."

"But?"

"I'm getting tired of the insinuations. I'm about to pop the next guy who smirks and comments on my arriving stag. I could quiet them down by appearing with a beautiful woman on my arm."

Cally had considered his decidedly unromantic proposal, and the hollow feeling it started in her stomach.

"Free food," he'd added.

It wasn't that kind of hollow feeling.

"Think of it as a chance to get dressed up without anyone's putting the make on you. I'll guard you as if you were my baby sister fresh from convent school."

Guard her from whom? Him or herself?

"I promised Dr. Curtis no more men," she said.

"Don't think of me as a man, think of me as a ticket to Lincoln Center."

He'd gotten her to laugh. Then he'd gotten her to say yes. He would never get her to stop thinking of him as a man.

The doctor tapped her pen on the desk. "Cally? Would you like to talk about it? Are you going on this date?"

"Yes, I'm going." She sat up straighter. "But on my terms. He knows all about our contract, and he respects that." Maybe too much, her heart whispered. "He claims a woman who's sworn off men is perfect for him. I won't begrudge him time for his career or expect constant attention. I have a life of my own."

"That's true. So why do I sense you're worried?"

Cally grimaced at the sound of her own sigh. She was being silly, adolescent, and insecure. She could handle Steve Rousseau. After all, she was the one who'd gone overboard with the kiss. He hadn't even thought enough of it to mention it again.

She looked into Martha Curtis's understanding gray eyes. "It's funny, but he's just like my wanted poster."

"So you told me."

"I mean in another way. He's perfect for me. He isn't going to push or expect more than I can give. He's completely uninterested."

What more could a woman want? she sighed.

Four

"I'm afraid I'm not an opera fan, Steve."

"Don't worry. We're here to schmooze."

"To what?"

"Network. Back-scratch." And make Cally Baldwin feel at ease in his company, Steve reminded himself.

They walked across the plaza at Lincoln Center. Banners snapped in the early February wind. Lights and the sound of voices cascaded out onto the smooth stones.

"When it comes to opera, I'm more likely to snooze," Cally whispered as they swept through the doors. "Wake me if I snore."

Steve chuckled. With her hand tucked in his arm he had every excuse to cup his hand over hers. And squeeze. And once, with a rush of daring he hadn't experienced since high school, to brush the side of his arm against the swell of her breast. "I can't imagine you snoring." It was the only thing associated with a bed that he hadn't imagined her doing. Thinking about Cally had become a full-time hobby.

At the coat-check room, he helped her out of her cape. The red satin lining made sensual whispers, reminding Steve of sheets and fantasies and more beds. Considering the effect her mere presence was having on his body, he thought crowds and public places were his best bet if he planned to maintain this pretense of wanting nothing more than a date.

With a handful of introductions to people he knew, they made their way to their seats and settled in for the first act. When that was over, he ushered her toward the lobby.

"What do you say we hit the buffet table? I promised you free food, as I recall."

"Lead the way."

He nodded over the crowd and placing his hands on her waist, steered Cally toward an even tighter knot of people.

"I feel like part of a two-person conga line," she retorted over her shoulder.

"Almost there. Excuse us. Excuse me. Brian, how're you doing? Excuse us."

After thirteen years in New York, Steve found crowds as natural as exhaust-filled air, traffic, and dodging messengers on bikes. Parting a crowd with Cally Baldwin gave it a whole new dimension—and she'd just given him an idea.

Dancing. Under what pretense could he take her dancing? Then he could wrap his arms around her and hold her, her body moving against his in rhythm, the slower the better.

"This must be the place." Cally came to a full stop as they reached the end of a line stretching far beyond a table laden with food.

Steve bumped into her, then jumped away. The evidence of his thoughts was becoming apparent. "Excuse me."

"Certainly." She glanced him up and down. One minute he was touchy/friendly, the next he was keeping the kind of distance a priest would approve of. "Are you okay?"

"Just don't want to crowd you."

Fine. Except Cally wasn't sure she wanted the distance. Close was kind of nice. Ironically, just as she began to feel comfortable with him near, he backed off. Right now he was looking hungrily at the hors d'oeuvres, the way she wanted him to look at her.

"Want some?"

"I shouldn't. I mean—" Cally tried to tuck a strand of hair behind her ear, only to find it pinned up with a comb. This was as innocuous as dates got. She was there as a friend, not a potential lover. Just because his touch had her longing for things he, she, and Dr. Curtis all knew she shouldn't have, didn't mean she had to go off the deep end.

"After the second act they're planning desserts and drinks in a private room," he explained.

Food again. Wasn't the old adage the way to a man's heart. . . ? Cally's heart was rapidly sinking. But why should it? She'd spent most of the week convincing herself she wasn't after his heart. And she was determined to spend the evening proving it.

The lights dimmed, the crowd shifted toward the theater, and they took their seats.

They had to share a program. Their heads bumped as they read. He pointed out some of the famous names. Cally nodded. A guffaw from another row distracted her. When she turned back, Steve's face was inches from hers.

"I, uh, what did you just say?"

He grinned. That was all. A slow, take-it-as-it-comes grin, the kind a man might grin when everything was coming his way. "I said that's a beautiful dress."

"Oh, thank you."

It was a black, scoop-neck, tight-fitting knit on top, with approximately eight layers of tiered black taffeta from the waist to the knees. Black stockings and black, strappy sandals completed her outfit.

The sartorial survey had taken him on a tour of territory he'd been trying to keep his eyes off all night. He was reminded of why when his gaze came back to hers. She looked as startled as a fawn, her large blue eyes peering into his, the way they had when he'd kissed her, just before she'd kissed him back—the way he wanted to kiss her right now.

"What are you thinking?" he asked softly.

"That I shouldn't be here."

"Don't like opera?" He patted his shoulder. "You get sleepy, just lean over."

She glanced down at his hand on the lapel of his dark suit, taking in the firm, blunt, elongated fingers with squared-off nails. His hands were those of a man who wouldn't mind a day's work, or a night's pleasure.

She swallowed, thanking the gods that be that he hadn't worn a tux. Steve Rousseau in a tux would be more than she could handle. Although she was handling this about as gracefully as a novice juggler with a half dozen plates spinning.

"At least you like the dress," she said, fiercely reminding herself why she was there. "That was the order, wasn't it? For a beautiful woman on your arm?"

His smile thinned. With a frisson of caution

Cally knew right then that he wasn't a man to toy with.

"I didn't mean to insult you," he said, his voice low. "Only to get you to come."

"Exactly." She refocused her attention on the stage. Maybe it'd be better for both of them if they kept their minds on opera. She flipped through the program, aware of his eyes burning a path down her profile.

She knew she was chattering, but it filled the yawning silence. As did the constant internal reminder to be herself. She didn't have to say the things he wanted to hear. "You know, opera puzzles me. I mean, what is the appeal of Viking women in bronze-plated D cups and horned helmets? If I met one in the ladies' room, I'd walk the other way. Fast. Those babes carry sticks!"

Steve tossed his head back and gave a shout of laughter. Heads turned as he grasped her hand and raised it to his lips. "I love your sense of humor, did I ever tell you that?"

Before Cally could recover, or even withdraw her hand, the second act started with a crash of cymbals. She jumped. Steve smiled and gently, almost paternally, set her hand back on the armrest. At least she now had an hour or so to think about this predicament. It would take at least that long for the sensation of his lips on her hand to fade away.

She focused on the stage, frantically making mental lists. She was there because (a) she liked him (b) couldn't say no, and (c) promised herself and Dr. Curtis she'd go out with a man and simply date. No high hopes. No pretending to be what she wasn't to impress him. No blinding herself to his faults. And Steve was the all-too-willing guinea pig for this test of her judgment.

She'd wasted no time noticing how respected he was by the people who knew him. They even seemed a little in awe of him. In this proper, conservative crowd, his hair was a trifle long. He wore it slicked back, giving the appearance of a fashionable rogue, a rebel who'd tamed enough of his impulses to get along in the button-down world. He had that whiff of danger, the unexpected. The looks of admiration the ladies sent his way only reaffirmed Cally's opinion.

But your judgment is dreadful, she chided herself. *You're too needy, too suspicious, you're not supposed to want anyone right now, you're—*

"Daydreaming?"

Cally blinked as the lights came up. She'd been caught staring at Steve instead of the falling curtain. "You sure this was a good idea?"

"One of the best I've had in years." He grinned. "Come on, let's get to that buffet before everyone else does. We probably have another hour or so of small talk before this breaks up."

They walked to a private room, where tall white walls were decorated with swaths of peachy fabric and tartan plaids shot through with threads of matching peach.

"Company colors," he murmured. "Don't ask me."

It looked like a uniform for a Catholic girls' school. "I wouldn't dream of it."

This room wasn't quite as jammed as the central lobby. A small group of people had gathered around a buffet table piled with desserts. That was exactly the direction in which Steve was steering her.

Butterflies invaded her stomach. First-time introductions were always the hardest.

"What's wrong?"

She'd come to a complete halt. Steve was pressed up behind her, but she didn't move. "Can we get some things clear here?" She swung around, the skirt of her dress brushing his knees.

He stepped back. "Such as?"

"I've been called honest to a fault, I just think you should know that. No matter how I pretend to like people, I do have this tendency to say what I think."

"Particularly when it comes to babes carrying sticks?"

"That too." At least he was laughing about it. "You might not think it's funny if I say the wrong thing in front of your boss."

"My boss can handle himself. Otherwise he wouldn't be boss. Besides, what makes you think I'd be low enough to bring you here simply to impress other people?"

"Your invitation, for starters."

"Yeah, well." Steve had approximately six strides in which to curse himself for this entire concept. The end might justify the means, but it certainly meant taking the long way around.

He stopped just short of the table for a quick briefing. "Cally, I like your company. But you won't have anything to do with me because of your contract, right? That's why I thought I'd invite you—"

Her eyes were growing guarded; that bothered him more than her ready-to-run look. She'd probably heard one too many unflattering confessions from the men she'd known. Steve quickly reconsidered. If this whole pretense was worth anything, he couldn't ditch it this fast. After all, it had worked so far. "I invited you here to . . ."

"Schmooze?"

"Right. That's all. As you said, you signed a contract."

"I did."

"And I'll stick by it."

Why *he* should stick by *her* agreement, Cally didn't completely understand, but Steve wasn't about to give her a chance to question him further. Faster than she could say "Glad to meet you," she plastered a smile on her face and extended her hand.

"Cally Baldwin, say hello to Walter Konig, CFO, and Martin MacKenzie, CEO of AmeriConGroup. And this is Madelyn—"

"Madelyn MacKenzie, CEW. Chief executive's wife."

"Cally Baldwin, UFO," Cally replied smartly. "Unidentified fluttering object." She flounced the tiered skirt of her black dress.

Everyone laughed. That didn't distract Cally from admiring Madelyn's jewels.

"You like these, dear?"

"They're beautiful. Talk about the lights of Manhattan. Are you sure they aren't lit by Con Ed?" Cally caught herself abruptly. "I'm sorry. I didn't mean to stare."

"Stare away! You think I wear them to be subtle? Marty likes me to show them off."

"By all means, young lady," her husband added. "No sense having the most beautiful wife in the world without letting her shine. I've always said she lit up my life." He looked at Madelyn as if she were a treasure.

With a start, Cally realized that was exactly the way Steve looked at her.

"And what do you do, dear?" Madelyn asked.

"I'm a researcher."

"At a laboratory?"

"A think tank."

"Good heavens, she'll probably be analyzing us all. 'The Place of the Party in Corporate Power Structures.' "

Cally had to admit the idea had occurred to her.

Madelyn took her arm. "You men stay here and talk business. We two are going to dish some dirt."

Steve gave Cally a helpless look as she was led away.

"Don't worry, dear, you'll have more fun with me," Madelyn asserted.

From behind, Steve's whisper followed her: "I can't contradict her there."

It was a joke. Perhaps it was the fact that it was meant only for them that made her heart skitter. Or maybe it was his breath on her cheek, the slight scrape of beard that lingered no matter how closely he shaved. Cally felt the burnish on her cheek long after Madelyn sat her down.

"So, Cally, tell me all about you, then tell me all about you and Steve."

"This is only the second time we've been out. Or third, if you count our first dinner together."

"I expect any evening with Steve Rousseau counts."

Cally weighed the remark. Improving her judgment about men meant being willing to gather information, good or bad. "Is he a real Casanova?"

"On the contrary." Peering across the room, Madelyn took a moment to formulate the thought.

"He's a private person who doesn't act private. He can charm those men all night, and they won't know one whit more about him at the end of the evening than when it began. Men don't know how to ask questions."

"That could be." Cally watched more closely. Steve was listening respectfully, saying little, taking in a lot.

"He's a mile ahead of every one of them," Madelyn said, "except Marty."

Cally glanced at the proud, eagle-eyed glint of the older woman. Madelyn smiled back. "Oh, I'm mighty proud of my Marty. And I'm holding on to him. No younger second wife for that CEO."

"I can't imagine he'd want one."

"That's the hard part, dear. Hard to know what men want when they so often don't know themselves."

It sounded wise, but Cally wasn't convinced. Steve seemed very sure of what he wanted. She was the one who was confused.

Steve reappeared with Cally's cape draped over his arm.

"Trying to rescue her before she's interrogated by experts, Steven?" Madelyn asked with a smile.

"The excuse I'd prepared was that Cally gets sleepy at the opera. I thought we'd step outside for some fresh air."

"At ten degrees above zero?" Cally questioned.

"Ought to wake anybody up."

"True," Cally murmured doubtfully.

"Wouldn't want me to have to carry you up your stairs and tuck you in bed," Steve murmured, bowing gallantly.

That quickly, Cally was standing. "Definitely not!"

He extended his arm. "Then, shall we?"

"You make a lovely couple, dear," Madelyn said, giving Steve a meaningful look, as if he were the one who needed to heed the message.

"Having a good time?" he asked once they were outside on the plaza.

Cally unkinked her neck with a roll of her shoulders. "A long evening, but fun."

Some of the orchestra members strolled by, instrument cases in hand. Taxis were forming a line at the curb.

Steve and Cally walked slowly, the sound of their heels keeping pace with the receding murmur of voices. His steps were low, deliberate. Her heels clicked.

"Tell me more about yourself." Steve rolled his eyes and laughed at his own inventiveness.

"Where should I start?"

"You're honest to a fault, you say. Unlike certain men you've met."

"I've told you all that?"

"I gathered that much from what's his name, Marlin."

"Being honest doesn't seem to attune me to it in others. You for instance."

He kept his face blank. "Ask me anything."

"You'll be honest?"

As long as she didn't ask why he kept inviting her out. "Ask away."

Given the opportunity, Cally chose her questions carefully. "Are you married?"

"Nope. Close once, not since."

"Are you gay?"

"Hardly."

"Don't be offended, just thought I'd ask."

"Hey, it's open season on personal questions. Go on."

"Do you believe in fidelity?"

"Completely."

"Does your idea of recreational activity include drugs?"

"A recreational beer is as wild as I get. Although sometimes I go off the deep end and insist on ale. Have I bored you yet?"

I haven't been bored for one minute since I met you, she thought.

"I'm also healthy as a horse, as fit as one of those fiddles."

She'd noticed.

"Any more questions?"

"Have you been completely honest with me?"

He paused. "Not entirely."

She came to a stop. "Disturbing, but honest." Cally sat on a low cement-block wall, wrapping her cape tightly around her. His simple dark suit was winter weight but not all-weather. He didn't seem to notice the snow swirling like dusting powder across the tips of his shoes. "You'll catch your death."

"I'm fine. Aren't you frigid?" A curse slipped out at his choice of words, although he followed it with laughter. "I meant, you must be freezing. That cape isn't thicker than a blanket, and you're not wearing gloves. Let me."

He took her hands, warming them briskly, keeping them tucked between his as he sat on the wall beside her.

"Speaking of capes, you seem very respected by your colleagues."

"How did we get onto this subject?"

"Madelyn referred to you as a boy wonder."

Steve grimaced. "Oh, that. I don't wear a cape; she must have seen me in my tights."

"You have quite a reputation, she says."

"Right, and the Wondermobile is in the shop, or I would have picked you up."

"I insisted on a cab, remember?"

"All right. I made a splash fresh out of business school, and no one has ever let me forget it. How's that?"

"And you've been working hard to live up to their expectations ever since."

"I see analysis has taught you something."

"Sorry."

"Speaking of that litany of questions you asked a moment ago, do you mind my concluding that you've dated some real winners?"

She shrugged.

"Bad enough to lead you to Dr. Curtis?"

"What do you think of her?" They'd come upon a topic Cally could be enthusiastic about.

Not Steve. Not when her contract with Dr. Curtis was keeping them apart. "I'd rather talk about us."

"That's a cliché." She smiled and turned her hand over in his, palm to palm.

Love at first sight was also a cliché, Steve thought as he looked deeply into her eyes, wondering if she saw it in his. How could he convince her he was the right man for her? All she had to do was let go of the past and he was there, waiting, ready.

She was also backing off imperceptibly. He loosened his grip on her hand.

"Maybe we could run down a list of your likes and dislikes," he said, forcing his voice into a casual tone. An underlayer of irritation remained.

"Likes?"

Despite the unexpected headiness of merely holding hands with the man and the soaring music still ringing in her ears and the harsh wind that should have snapped her out of it, Cally couldn't think of anything she liked more than sitting there with him.

Getting no answer to his innocuous question, Steve prompted her. "Like those? Fur coats." He indicated two women waiting for a taxi. Tawny had always been favorably impressed by expensive gifts.

Cally shook her head firmly. "Don't like them. The one on the right looks like road kill, the other could be Portuguese water spaniel."

Steve raised an eyebrow, trying to picture it.

"Seriously. That tight curly coat. It'd be very water resistant. Not too safe in Central Park, though."

"It would attract thieves?"

"No, it'd probably retrieve ducks."

This time Steve laughed loud enough to turn the ladies' heads. "Uh-oh. I know the one on the left. She's married to someone in Marketing. Lives in an Upper East Side brownstone filled with objects d'art."

"Where money is no object, art is?"

"Kind of like that, yeah." Steve did a double take. "You are on the honest side."

"Personality flaw, remember? Want to go back in?"

He shrugged. "You set all the limits."

True. Silently, she thanked him for reminding her. "Steve, since we're talking about honesty and limits—"

"You're married."

"No," she scolded. "I've had very bad luck with men. Not bad luck, bad choices. I'm not ready for anything more than evenings like this right now."

"Great."

He didn't have to sound so enthusiastic about it. "Great?"

"Sure. That means you'll come to the Knicks game with me a week from Sunday."

"Knicks," she repeated dryly.

"You don't like basketball?"

"Actually, I love it."

"A woman who takes sports seriously."

"You sound as if you don't believe me." She took a deep breath. "Their guards are better than ever, although slow on the post-up, which is amazing considering they were drafted for speed. Their center is playing at seventy-five percent due to bone-spur surgery. The forwards have yet to live up to last year's rebounding stats, however, they are playing the Pistons Sunday, and I wouldn't miss it for the world."

"In other words, you like basketball."

"Didn't I just say that?" She batted her lashes coquettishly. "Still inviting me?"

"Yes."

"And this isn't a real date?"

Steve thought fast. He also made decisions fast. It was not knowing which answer to give that made him pause. "Company function. I'm treating six group leaders from my department, along with their spouses, to tickets on the twenty-yard line."

"And I get to play escort again. Not too romantic, Steve."

"Should I get down on one knee and publicly

ask you to a Knicks game?" He proceeded to do so.

"No!" Jumping up, Cally brushed snow off his knee. Realizing how personal she was getting, she backed away just as quickly. "I'll come."

"Not a very romantic acceptance, but I'll take it." Giving her hands a brisk rubdown, he blew on them. Then he brought them to his lips. "You're freezing."

Not on the inside. Cally's heart was pounding, her ears ringing, the lights of Lincoln Center glittering in the background. But starting somewhere around her toes and making its way up was fire, slow, liquid, melting fire.

"Cally?"

"Yes?" Her voice was a shuddering whisper.

"It's a stress fracture."

"What is?" she asked dreamily.

"Their center is out with a fracture, not a bone spur."

"Oh." If she needed confirmation that her voice had completely escaped her, she could see it hanging in a misty puff of air between them. "Are we going to argue?"

He moved in closer. "Hardly."

"Steve?"

"Yes?"

"There is no twenty-yard line in basketball."

He grinned in spite of himself. "I was wondering when you'd start paying attention."

Oh, but she was—to the smell of his aftershave, the aura of warmth he exuded, the animal energy revealed in his stride as he led her toward the street. His steps aligned with hers so their bodies never lost contact. One of his arms was around her waist, the other raised to hail a cab.

She felt his ribs when he moved, realizing her hand was inside his jacket. When he looked down at her, his face was in shadow cast by the lights behind them.

She was paying attention, all right, to all the wrong, dangerous, seductive things about Steve Rousseau. Like the way his head tilted and his lips parted, the sound of his whispering her name just before his mouth came down on hers.

Five

His lips were sweet, flavored by the icing of a rum cake he'd snatched from the buffet. It was a taste Cally wanted to savor.

She felt as if her blood were a thick, heavy liquid, a liqueur perhaps, something dark and licorice. Could she be drunk on nothing more than the taste of rum cake?

He pulled his mouth away. "Are you getting cold?" He sounded rushed, intense.

She shivered, but not from the cold. The man made his own heat wave. Her hands twined inside his jacket, feeling him tense as the cold penetrated his shirt. Cally wanted to make him jump like that when he wore no shirt at all, when her tongue found a nipple and pressed.

In the meantime, her palms investigated the rustle of cotton, the muscle beneath it, the blades of his back and the way they moved when his arms went around her for another, deeper kiss. In a corner of her mind, Cally knew they were making a spectacle of themselves in a very public place. Every other part of her was past caring.

Steve clenched her shoulders in his hands. "Cal. The taxi's here." His voice was harsh.

Funny, Cally thought, that they should both be losing their voices. So much was being said, but not with words. She laughed softly, purring against the side of his neck. He tensed again.

"The hell with it," he muttered, waving the driver away. Someone else could have the taxi. He was going to have Cally. He bent his head till their foreheads were touching. "You like that?" he asked, his voice thick.

"Mmm-hmm."

She didn't hold back. Steve found that the most exciting thing about her. For all her fears and doubts, when she kissed, she was all there.

He knew he should be the one to stop, especially since his whole plan hinged on pretending he didn't care, wouldn't expect anything from her. Hell, at this point, what he expected involved loving her till dawn, and watching her bear his children and share his life for the next forty years.

So why was he parting her cape and tugging her closer? It couldn't all be due to her mouth on his neck, the groan of pure pleasure she elicited. When she touched him with her tongue, he shuddered like a subway platform.

"We always say good-bye this way, don't we?" she murmured dreamily.

"It's becoming a bad habit." He groaned.

"We wouldn't necessarily have to say goodnight."

She didn't have to raise her voice, not with her mouth beside his ear. When she dipped her tongue into it, he lost his voice completely, the voice that should have been saying no.

All he could think of was her mouth. A dark, luscious red, it was where he could see it now, curving in a sexy, sassy smile. Unfortunately for his self-control, her body leaned into him as she tilted her head back to look up at him. Her breasts brushed his chest. Only his shirt, her cape, and her thin black dress separated them.

Inside the cape, he ran his fingertips down her bare neck. His hands were cold, too, adding to the sensations that were making them tremble. Tracing the pale slope, he drew the material off her shoulder. It was clingy, like a leotard. He doubted it had a zipper. The whole thing could be lowered in one piece, baring her skin, her breasts.

For the sake of his sanity, he stopped. He wouldn't brush his lips against her shoulder or taste the tang of her skin. He couldn't.

Her mouth skimmed his neck again. Not fair. She was eating him up, and he was stiff as a lamppost. That applied to more than his spine. "Cally, babe, we've got to stop."

She moaned like a kitten woken from a deep sleep, her mouth nuzzling against his earlobe. Would she make sounds like that in bed? His pulse rocketed another notch.

A taxi appeared.

Steve stepped back to swing open the door. Giving Cally's address to the driver, he handed a ten through the hinged opening in the Plexiglas divider.

Cally scooted across the seat and looked up at him. It took everything he had not to get in. "I'll call you about the game," he said, his voice rasping like a steel file. He shut the door between them.

"Steve!"

"Babe. Don't make it harder." It was already as hard as it got. He reached in through the open window, cupping her face, touching her hair. He pulled an ornamental comb free and watched a cascade of dark hair fall to her shoulders. He clenched his fists as he pictured running his hands through it, spreading it over a pillow, letting it drape over the side of a rumpled, thoroughly used bed.

He slapped the side of the door. "Go ahead!"

The taxi took off. Thrusting his hands into his pockets, he concentrated on the comb pricking his palm. He stepped off the curb to watch the red taillights fade out of sight. An inch of watery slush closed over his shoes.

"Idiotic" was the nicest word he chose to define his predicament. For the sake of his plan, he'd let her leave, actually sent her away. She was an adult, offering, willing, wanting. He could have had her for the asking.

And lost her in the morning.

At least, that's what he tried telling himself, until pictures of Cally Baldwin, in bed, in the morning, caused him more torment than this second-guessing.

He didn't want to be another of her mistakes. They both had to be ready. He'd done the gentlemanly thing. As he sat morosely in the next cab that came along, flexing his soggy toes, his language was far from gentlemanly.

"I don't know what happened," Cally said, clutching a tissue in her hand. "One minute we were, uh, saying good-night, the next he was trundling me off in a taxi. Alone."

"Did you want to be alone?" Dr. Curtis asked gently.

"Does anyone?" Wonderful answer. Nice and

abstract. "Am I rushing into things from fear of being alone?"

"You'd have to answer that for yourself, Cally. Although you do seem to need a man in your life. Have you considered why?"

She'd been too busy aching for Steve Rousseau. One minute he'd been clutching her as if he'd never let her go, the next literally driving her away. At least he was honorable enough to abide by her rules. Even if *she'd* dispensed with them at the first kiss.

"The moment I decide to swear off men, I start dating a man I can't wait to take home."

"You mean have sex with?"

"If you're going to resort to euphemisms, I'm leaving," Cally retorted.

Martha smiled indulgently. "Is it sex you're after?"

"I've never been one for one-night stands, if that's what you mean." Cally stared at the carpet. "But this man . . ." She shook her head firmly. "No, that's not it. He's more than willing to respect my rules."

"No men?"

"That was the contract, wasn't it?"

"We seem to be back to the question of why you can't stay away from him."

"Maybe it's like a diet. The minute you can't have food, you binge worse than ever."

The doctor wasn't laughing. "Do you feel out of control, Cally?"

"Only when he kisses me." It was an honest answer. It was the reason behind it that stumped her—but not as much as Steve's behavior. "Wouldn't any normal man jump at the chance to take me home?"

"Possibly. Not all men are after sex."

"Only the ones I've dated," Cally replied with a wry grin. "This one waits until I'm willing, then sends me away!"

"Maybe he wants more."

"In my wildest dreams."

"You don't trust him?"

"I don't trust men in general."

"That's a sweeping statement."

Cally looked down sheepishly. "I don't trust myself. That's the real answer. So what am I getting into here? Am I in over my head? Clutching at straws?" The tissue was a crushed wad. Getting up to pace, Cally banked it off the wall and into the wastebasket. Two points.

"I'm seeing him on Sunday. A basketball game."

"A date?"

"Another public function."

"Is that what you want?"

"I wish you'd stop asking me that."

"It's my job to get you to face things that are uncomfortable. We still need to find out why you feel it necessary to go against your own wishes and break the contract."

"Because he's everything I ever wanted. A walking wanted poster."

"Well." Dr. Curtis sighed, screwing the cap on her pen and closing the manila folder. "If he's everything you want, then I wish you both a long and happy marriage." She stood.

Cally sat down with a plop. "You know that isn't going to happen!"

"Why not?"

"Because it won't work! It never works. When it comes to men, something always goes wrong."

"Such as?"

"I make mistakes, or I pick someone who's bound to leave me, or use me."

"Like your new friend?"

"No." She knew with absolute faith that Steve wasn't using her. He took her on public dates because he wanted to see her. She'd seen through the "just an escort" ruse almost from the beginning. And she wanted to see him. But she was afraid of the risks of getting involved. "I've never felt this way about a man. That's the scary part. I feel as if I'm on the edge of something, and I don't want to ruin it."

"And he's not pressuring you."

"Just the opposite."

"Okay," the doctor said soothingly. "It might be better if you slowed things down for a couple weeks. You've already laid the groundwork, you're always surrounded by people—"

"I can get my feet wet without going whole hog."

"To mix metaphors, yes. If you have to see him how about for lunch, something with a time frame, so you don't get carried away? That way you can get by while I'm gone."

"Gone?" Cally cried in dismay.

"St. Croix for two weeks every February. But don't worry. Keep it light. You say he's been good about respecting your wishes. State them firmly the next time you see him. And no *good-night kisses.*"

State it firmly. Cally sat in her office practicing telling Steve exactly what she wanted. With no weekly pep talks from Martha Curtis, she was on her own.

"No more good-night kisses," she hissed, flipping through a pile of articles submitted for the next *Policy Issues*. She didn't care what kind of manners his mother had instilled in him, this time she'd see herself to the taxi.

Hands shaking, she picked up the phone and called him to ask him to lunch. She was making the first move this time. A basketball game, surrounded by his coworkers, was a safe setting for a date, but it was no place to lay down rules. After repeating his name to three different levels of secretaries, she learned he was in a meeting. "Yes, I'd like to leave a message."

Two hours and four business-related phone calls later, the phone rang. With two volumes of *International Seagoing Precedents* stuffed under her arm, Cally wobbled atop the ladder, reaching for the highest shelf in her cluttered office. The portable phone rang again, startling her from its place on the top shelf. "So that's where you've been hiding!" she exclaimed. A piece of paper fluttered to the floor, released from her clenched lips.

Tucking volume three between her knees as a temporary holding place, she answered on the second ring. "Research," she chirped, holding the phone between her shoulder and ear.

"Cally."

"Steve." The ladder wobbled again.

"Recognized me on one word. I'm flattered. Got your message."

Cally left her volumes on the top rung of the ladder and trundled down. She glanced at her office clock, a cat with rhinestone eyes and a waving tail, a gag gift from her colleagues last Christmas. Its whiskers read two o'clock.

"I got so busy with work, I forgot I'd called." It was mostly true, she chided herself. She had lost track of time.

"What did you want?"

He was more businesslike on the phone. To the point. She took the hint.

"I wanted to have lunch. A little late for that today." No reason for her to feel so relieved.

"Not at all. I haven't eaten yet. Meeting ran long."

"Couldn't you send out for sandwiches?"

"Not for six people in six different countries doing a conference call."

"I thought McDonald's was international."

He chuckled. "Not for this bunch. How about you?"

"Me? Haven't had a bite, unless you count the raspberry-jam doughnut I had for breakfast."

Steve wanted to say something about her ruining her figure, but he wasn't sure he wanted to think about her figure while he was in the office. He'd been acting distracted enough lately. "Tell you what, pumpkin. Do you have a private office?"

"Will a book-strewn cubbyhole do?"

"Close enough. See you in half an hour."

Cally set down the phone. Pumpkin? He had to be kidding. Could she really sneak out at two-thirty for lunch? Maybe she could claim she was going over to the main library for more materials. She did that often enough. She'd meet him out front—

"No, Cally," she warned herself. No sneaking around to see a man. But the alternative was his coming there. She raced around neatening the piles of papers and stacks of books. Three fast-food bags from the previous week hit the wastebasket. Who'd have thought research was an orderly business?

Just then a senior partner appeared with three articles he wanted her to go over. Deadline work. She nodded as if that were exactly what she'd been wanting to tackle, knowing she'd be taking it home if she ever hoped to finish it in time for the March edition of the *Policy Issues.*

"Hope you like fried chicken."

Cally looked up from her desk. On the outer edges of the light cast by her brass desk lamp, she could see Steve lounging in the doorway. The cat winked at her, two-thirty on the dot.

"I didn't even give you directions."

"Columbia's easy to find." He shrugged, inviting himself in. Scanning the mounds of paper on her desk, in the in-baskets, in the out-baskets, and stacked on the floor, he decided Dickensian was the best adjective to describe her office. "Crowded enough for you?"

It was considerably more crowded with him there. Cally was aware of the dust stirred up by the old furnace kicking on somewhere four floors below. That had to be why she was suddenly so flushed, warm, and breathless. She wanted to open a window. Only when she was standing did she remember her office didn't have one. She snapped out of it and put on a smile.

"Have a seat, please."

"You do like fried chicken?" He looked doubtful.

"Sure!"

"I picked it up from an Indian place on the corner. Knew I'd find something up this way."

Cally gulped. The Indian place on the corner was notorious for its spices.

Seeing her coat on a hook by the door, Steve

draped his over the back of a wood-slat chair and pulled it up to her desk, keeping the massive steel contraption between them. That ought to be safe enough for both of them.

They each took a bag and began doling out napkins and plastic ware, investigating the contents of white cardboard boxes.

"Great idea," Steve said.

"Thanks. I can't say I expected you to rush right over, but I'm glad you did."

"So'm I."

"How's the weather?" Lord, she couldn't keep it any more innocuous if she tried.

"Fine. Warm for mid-February."

"I noticed the raincoat."

She noticed everything he was wearing. Only the *Policy Issues'* biggest benefactors wore suits as well tailored as his.

Cally took a deep breath and folded her hands on the desk. "The reason I called you here today, Steve—" She glanced up, so did he. They both laughed.

Steve wiped his mouth with a napkin and grimaced. "Are we that formal?"

"Well, I guess, in a way, yes. I was hoping we could keep things a little more formal from now on."

He eyed her for a few minutes, picking the meat off a chicken bone with even white teeth. Then he licked his lips.

A tumbling sensation somewhere below her heart had her wondering if he was doing that on purpose.

He dropped the bone in a box they'd set aside for leftovers. "Does this mean you're canceling Sunday?"

"No, I said I'd go."

"And with grim determination and gritted teeth, you will. Is that it?"

She frowned. "You're exaggerating."

And you're running, he thought to himself. He cursed just as silently. Even though she'd been the one doing most of the kissing Saturday night, he hadn't stopped her. Now she was scared. If he wasn't careful, she'd run, and that'd be the last he'd see of her.

"How formal?" he asked.

She sighed and unclenched her folded fingers. "No good-night kisses." Who'd have guessed simple self-preservation could sound so silly? If he dared laugh, she'd brain him with the curry sauce.

He didn't. He considered thoughtfully. Picking up a container, he offered her the contents. "Last piece?"

"No thanks."

"Don't mind if I do." He took his time over another chicken leg. "I can live with that."

Her shoulders sagged with relief. She wouldn't stand a chance in poker, Steve thought. She was so transparent sometimes. With that, he pictured a game of strip poker. She'd lose. He straightened in the chair, clearing his throat and reaching across the desk to shake her hand. "It's a deal."

"Deal," she said, smiling.

His heart clutched in his chest, and he forced himself to go easy on the handshake. Her smile was beautiful. In the pool of light cast by the desk lamp, her eyes were dark and inviting. "For now," he said, his voice low, determined, his hand still wrapped around hers.

The tense moment was broken by a woman's

bustling through the door with an armload of newspapers that reached nearly to her chin. She slapped down three for Cally. "*London Times*, Paris *Herald Tribune*, *Roma*—oh."

"Cordelia, this is Steve Rousseau."

"Hi, Steve." Cordelia shook hands from under the pile, then quickly turned her attention back to Cally. "Stonewall Jackson says there's an article in the *Trib* about drought-relief efforts as a way of undermining socialism in sub-Saharan nations. Thinks you should pick up on that."

"I'll take a look."

"What are you eating? Smells like that stuff they sell down the street."

"Bye, Cordelia."

Cordelia's eyes grew wide at Cally's firm tone. Backing out of the door, she gave Steve the once-over. "Bye."

"Good-bye." He turned to Cally, smiling. "Stonewall Jackson?"

"The boss."

He reached into his inner pocket to put on a pair of glasses. "You read all these?"

"Any political news." She loved him in those glasses. She liked glasses, period. They made women look smart and men look sensitive. On the outside. She reminded herself she barely knew the man sitting across from her scanning the *Times*' financial page.

"Steve?"

"Yes?" He smiled apologetically and folded the paper. "The markets never sleep."

"Tell me about your parents. When you were a kid. Any brothers and sisters?"

He accepted the interrogation graciously. "Two of each. Mom stayed home playing Mrs. Cleaver.

Seriously. She wore a dress and a strand of pearls to do housework. As Dad got more successful, she had a maid do the housework, but the strand of pearls stayed."

"What did your dad do?"

"Built a retail carpet company. From scratch. One of the biggest in New Jersey."

"Rousseau's Rugs? I remember hearing their commercials on the radio when I was a kid!"

"They hit hard times during the Iran crisis. Persian rugs got scarce for a while. He sold out to a multinational corporation, and he and Mom retired to Palm Springs."

"So you had the ideal nuclear family."

"For that day and age. Dad was big on the work ethic, bringing home the paycheck. He fell a little short on being around for us kids, but that's the way it was then."

"And now you're the one working all hours?"

"Only because I don't have a family to devote my time to. That would change, Cally."

She lowered her gaze and scooped up a spoonful of rice. Only the Indian place on the corner would consider rice a natural accompaniment for fried chicken.

"How about your family?" he asked.

"Just Mom and me."

"Your father. . . ?"

"Dead. No, gone."

"There's a difference there," he said quietly.

"He left when I was nine."

"Then you must remember him."

"Better than he remembers me, I think. He tried to keep in touch, whenever Mom called him and told him it was my birthday or the holidays were coming up. He moved a lot. We never did.

Somehow Mom was always able to find him, for my sake. When I was fifteen, I told her to stop bothering."

"Sounds tough."

Cally shrugged. "Don't let me bore you with the broken-home blues. Mom and I made it okay. I came to terms with that a long time ago."

"Did you?"

"I don't *think* I hold any grudges against men. Why? Do you think I should talk it over with Dr. Curtis? Speaking of which, weren't you supposed to see her again?"

"She's gone. Two weeks—"

"—two weeks in St. Croix," they said in tandem.

Steve laughed. "I have one more session to go over my profile. Are you still seeing her?"

"She said six weeks should do it, but sometimes I wonder if we don't have a lot further to go."

How much longer would he have to wait? Steve wondered. He glanced at the clock and did a double take as the cat winked off the seconds. "Guess I should get going." He made no move to leave.

"Thanks for coming by." She didn't move either. Just looked at him for a few more minutes. She'd enjoyed this, she really had. With people walking up and down the hall, the sounds of voices calling back and forth between offices, the whir of the copy machine just outside her door, they'd had no privacy. Without the specter of hormones getting in the way, she'd been able to simply enjoy his company. Very much.

Scanning the hallway, Steve stood for a long moment in the doorway. Cally came up beside him. She immediately extended her hand. "See you Sunday."

He nodded, his gaze never leaving hers. He took her hand in his, but refused to shake it. He merely held it, palm to palm, then stepped through the doorway and started down the hall. "I'll pick you up," he called.

At the sound of an unfamiliar voice a few heads peeked out of office doors.

Cally realized she'd followed him partway down the hall. As he disappeared down the stairs she caught sight of herself in a glass door. She was wrapped in a stretched-out, oversize sweater that hung to midthigh, covering a long skirt and ankle boots with navy knee socks. It was warm attire for this musty old building, it was also suitable for running across to the college library at a moment's notice. "Oh, no!" she wailed.

"Get a load of that article in *Roma*?" Gerry Spender asked in response to her cry.

"I look like something from *Les Misérables*!"

"Oh." He adjusted his own glasses, bumping them up his nose. "Uh, well, I dunno. You look like you normally look. Doesn't she, Ben?"

That was all she needed, an appraisal of her looks from the fourth-floor research staff, all of whom were now standing in their doorways. "Oh, never mind! I'm going to the library," she muttered, "to hide in the stacks."

However, by the time five o'clock came around, Cally was back to congratulating herself on how well she'd handled Steve's visit. She'd been dignified and up-front about her needs. Above all, she'd stayed out of his arms. At last she'd conquered that distressing habit of melting like a snow sculpture on a sunny day every time he was around.

Despite lugging home an oversize bag full of

papers, she decided to step off the bus a few blocks early to enjoy the snow that had fallen while she'd been cooped up in bookstacks.

She looked down her street of converted brownstones. Summers might simmer, and rain turned scraps of discarded paper into soggy lumps on the sidewalk, but a fresh coat of snow could make her fall in love with New York all over again.

Laughing, she let her head fall back as flakes landed on her cheeks. She even stuck her tongue out to catch one. Yes, falling in love was exactly what it felt like.

"You know what's in that snow?" a gravelly voice said. "Sulfuric acid."

Cally brought her head out of the clouds to glare at the man who ran the newsstand. "Evening, George." She smiled.

Her mild greeting had no effect on his harangue.

"And mercury, and Lord knows what all. It floats in from Jersey, you know, from the chemical plants. People have all these wonderful ideas about snow, about how white and pure it is. 'Pure as the driven snow,' they say. But look at this, along the curb here. That's what snow is in New York. I wouldn't be eating that stuff."

She dug into her pocket for change to buy a *Post*. "Thanks, George, just what I needed to hear."

Six

Two weeks went by. The basketball game was a
memory, a very fond one. Cally and Steve had
stood near a concession stand eating hot dogs
and sipping soda, talking through the second
quarter until the halftime crowds had forced
them back to their seats. Cally had wondered
where her dedication to sports had gone. Days
later she'd tried to remember what they'd talked
about. It didn't seem to matter, except that she
was happy every time she recalled it.

Then there was the visit to the Museum of Mod-
ern Art. Their excuse was a two-hour seminar on
the international art market, which concerned
Steve for some reason. Her excuse was the politics
of culture versus capitalism. Did that justify an
entire afternoon cruising the Picassos, holding
hands through the Jasper Johns? Bantering and
trading art-talk like longtime friends?

Cally hoped that's what they were becoming.
All she had to do was keep her hormones under
control.

What would she tell Martha Curtis when she
saw her again? Yes, she and Steve were dating.
Sooner or later he would run out of public places
for them to meet. Yes, he held her hand. It started
when they walked down the street, him insisting

hands were warmer than gloves, body heat and all that. Kisses were still out. On that he'd respected her request.

But a niggling feeling remained, so small a voice she could barely hear it. The one that said kisses would be nice. The one that deflated like a balloon each time Steve bowed with a flourish and said good-night.

It was hardly worth mentioning to Dr. Curtis—that is, if she ever went back.

She was keeping her eyes open this time. If the slow pace was a bit frustrating, if occasionally she wished Steve would make a move . . . Cally decided to put off her next appointment until she had something more to say.

Then Steve stopped calling.

"I'm sorry, Miss Baldwin," the secretary said, "but he's been out all week."

"Out?" He could have told her he was going out of town. She shook off the thought. That was how clinging began, and the fear of being left. This was not an exclusive relationship. It barely was a relationship.

"He's so rarely sick," the secretary continued. "He may be out the week."

"Sick!" He *definitely* should have told her.

The crock of cream-of-potato soup was warm but heavy. Cally identified herself to the guard as someone from Steve's office. He allowed her up at once. The hallway was pristine and smelled of new carpet. The whole building smelled new. Stylish brass numbers identified each door. She knocked lightly on Steve's door, and it was flung open.

"About time. I've been looking for something to do—Cally!"

He looked shocked. He looked terrible. With a four-day growth of beard he had all the charm of a porcupine rousted out of hibernation. She'd expected silk pajamas. She got sweatpants tied at the waist with a ratty string tie and a college T-shirt with the sleeves cut off. He was clearly sick, barefoot, and grumpy as a bear.

"Your secretary said you'd been under the weather."

"Under it? It's been jumping up and down on me wearing army boots."

Cally tried to hide a smile. "Awwww," she cooed, rubbing his cheek, which rasped like heavy-grade sandpaper. "You don't enjoy being sick." He also didn't enjoy being teased, not in this mood.

"Makes a helluva lot of sense. Know anyone who does?"

"No, but some people enjoy being babied. Let's see about you."

He grumbled and waved her through the foyer. "I expected someone from the office. I've been going nuts with nothing to do."

She noted the magazines and newspapers strewn all over the floor by the sofa. He looked as if he'd saved and poured over every piece of junk mail one person could receive in a week. The long glass coffee table was littered with cups, plates, his glasses, a TV remote control, and a dozen crumpled tissues. Aside from that, it looked like a Manhattan high rise from *Better Homes and Gardens.*

"You have a beautiful apartment!"

"It makes a great sickroom," he groused.

Adopting the same sympathetic tone she would use for a six-year-old whose hamster had just died, she asked, "Steve, level with me. Is it Mongolian death flu?"

"They've identified it?"

"Mmm-hmm. But there is a cure." She lifted the lid on her prize. "Cream-of-potato soup, still steaming. I went light on the spices, and heavy—"

Heavy seemed the operative word, judging from the way Steve closed his eyes and steadied himself against the doorframe. "Think I'll pass."

"Or pass out!" She rapidly steered him toward the couch, the crock tucked in the crook of her arm. "Come on. Sit down."

Scowling, he pulled his arm free and shuffled toward the sofa under his own power.

She plumped a pillow and sat beside him.

Studying the dark brown crock while the room steadied, Steve decided soup didn't sound so bad. He'd eaten little else but broth and toast for four days, as evidenced by the half dozen paper plates littered with old crusts, and he was getting tired of getting off the couch to make that.

Cally was busy picking them up, gathering crumpled napkins. Her cheeks were bright, her smile as infectious as, as Mongolian death flu.

"You sure you want to be here? I could be contagious."

"I'm never sick a day in the winter." She had to explain why she was there. She didn't want him leaping to any conclusions about her waiting for his calls. She made it sound perfectly reasonable. "I was surprised you didn't call, so I tried your office."

He'd wanted to call her. Many a night he'd reached for the phone, only to realize he'd drifted off to sleep and it was one in the morning, or three. "I didn't want you to see me like this. I'm not Prince Charming when I'm sick or out of work."

He hated being away from the office.

"Damn secretary," he muttered.

"Oh?" Cally was busying herself in the living room. Obviously he'd abandoned the bedroom for the sofa all week

"I tell her to messenger over some work so I can stay busy, and she just chirps into the phone about how a full week of rest is in order."

"Sounds sensible to me. You don't have to work all the time."

"What else is there?"

"Well, Mr. Rousseau, there is more to life than work."

He growled again.

"There's your health."

Did she have to be so damn perky? "And what good does it do if I can't use it to work?"

"There's this." She held up a copy of *Playboy*.

From the entire stack of business and news-magazines he'd compiled, why'd she have to find that, much less wave it around. "A lot of good that does me when I'm dying."

"There's *moi*."

He wished. Another growl turned into a hacking cough. His throat felt as if it had been scoured. So did his face when he ran a hand across it. "I must look like—"

"Steve," she reproved gently. "Except for the ambience of a porcupine hovel, the dark circles under your eyes, and that perpetual scowl, you look as appealing as any death-row inmate. Now, is there anything you feel up to eating?"

"My socks."

Cally bit her cheek. "Coated tongue?"

"Made from the same camel-hair coat the man in the subway sleeps in." The woman had the temerity to laugh. He grimaced and looked up.

"You *are* a grump."

"Clear out while you can." The offer was made. He held his breath for a moment fearing she'd accept. He shouldn't have bothered. Standing in the bedroom doorway, hands on hips, she paid no attention at all.

"You need some fresh sheets. Is there a linen closet in here?"

He didn't even have to give her directions; a weak wave and she was gone.

Steve leaned his head back on the sofa cushions. He felt awful. Lying in front of the UN and letting tour buses drive over him couldn't have caused more aches. So why did having Cally there make such a difference? It was as if life was worth living again. Worth making an effort to at least smile when she came back in the room.

She pulled open the curtains and froze. She'd suspected the view of New York would be breathtaking. "This is wonderful!"

Steve merely grunted. He didn't need to see New York, it was Cally who lit up the room.

She turned to him. "A couch is no place to be when you're sick."

Neither was this town. Game shows and Spanish-language soap operas had been his companions for four days. He couldn't remember the last time he'd been so alone. Probably those first few months after Tawny left. He hadn't called Cally in a week. But he'd missed her, with an ache entirely new to patients with Mongolian death flu.

"Am I going to get you into bed?"

That won her a grin. "Good question," he replied.

Just friends. She'd rehearsed it all the way over. She was too aware of her pulse rippling beneath her skin every time she was around him. She was determined not to throw herself into anything with Steve Rousseau, much less a king-size bed. *If* he wanted more, he'd have to make the first move. And if she wasn't ready, she could always say no. He'd respect her limits, he had so far.

Besides, what could be safer than a man in the throes of the flu?

"Incredible apartment. I love all this white."

The kitchen was open with a counter separating it from the spacious living room. Groupings of furniture separated the room into a desk area and a living area with a dining set under the windows. The master bedroom was the only other room.

"I think it has all the style of an ice cream carton," Steve stated, his eyes following her every move. "White walls, white carpet, no architectural detailing."

"You have a guard in the lobby, that's nice."

"He's there to make sure no individuality gets in. You, for instance." She was a veritable beacon of freshness in this antiseptic place.

Her sweater was a teal-blue pullover. A white tank top under it kept the low V from revealing too much when she bent over to fluff another pillow for him. He knew she'd had a coat on when she came in. If he'd offered to hang it up, he'd forgotten.

She extended her hand. "Now, will you let me get you into bed?"

He considered a hundred comebacks, most of them similar to "If only . . ." "You were in the bedroom awhile. Preparing something special?" He tried to make it suggestive. It came out as a croak.

"I remade your bed." Why did that have to sound so intimate? Cally wondered. "Fresh sheets."

"Ahhh. Will you be joining me?"

He leaned on her arm for the short journey, but mostly to be near her. His legs felt unsteady. And he had this nagging feeling of gratitude to deal with, not to mention the unreasonable joy. When he was around her, his feelings seemed as unreliable as his body.

"Dizzy?"

"A little light-headed." It had to be that. Just being near a woman had never made his knees weak. He put his arm around her shoulders, his face near her hair. He wanted to kiss her, to hold her closer. But he looked, and probably smelled, terrible. She felt sorry for him. Kindheartedness had brought her there, nothing else. "You smell good."

"Thanks."

"From what little I can smell."

She laughed. "Thanks again." They began moving toward the bedroom. Fortunately, he wasn't as weak as he'd seemed at first. In fact, beneath the T-shirt his muscles were ropy and hard. His body smelled of man, but Cally could overlook that. She attributed the warmth of his skin to a touch of fever. And the warmth of hers?

"My apartment—" she began.

"Which you've never invited me up to."

"—which I've never invited you up to, is prewar."

"Very desirable." Like a few other things he could name.

"That means oak woodwork in the living room, wood floors, and a radiator that clatters something awful. Sometimes I swear the Man in the Iron Mask is being held prisoner in the basement. Wait." She looked up at him in shock. "Was that a smile?"

"Rigor mortis is setting in." He sat heavily on the edge of the bed. "Tell me more about your apartment. You have plants?" He'd pictured her as a plant person.

"About twenty. I have this reputation. People drop their plants off to be saved by me."

"Then I'm lucky you came by. I've been a vegetable since Sunday night."

Her laughter alone could cure a man.

"In addition to the plants, I have two bedrooms—"

"Two?"

"One's a spare, piled with books."

"As if you don't have enough in that office of yours."

"These are fiction. I also have a tiny L-kitchen with a view of the brick building next door, approximately three feet away."

" 'New York, New York.' "

"You're not going to sing are you?"

"I don't want to make you sick too."

She'd pulled the sheets down and expected him to raise his legs so she could tuck him in. "It's just typical," he said, "the brick view. People are so isolated in this town. Walled off and lonely." Steve looked up sheepishly, tugging the sheet roughly up over his sweats. "Didn't mean to get maudlin."

She was quiet for a minute, thoughtfully considering the blue of his eyes. She wasn't lonely in this apartment. Not at all. It was just the two of them in a city of millions.

"This ought to cheer you up." Crossing the room to pull on a magenta rope, Cally parted the curtains. Sunlight poured in.

"Torture me!" Steve threw a hand over his eyes.

"You need light."

"Like a vampire needs sunshine. Just give me a silver bullet and put me out of my misery."

"Sorry, I left my gun at home." She was standing at the foot of the bed. Steve wanted her to sit down again.

"I like your hair that way."

"This? The taxi window was stuck open, so it's blown all over." She played with a pearl comb to hold it off one cheek.

"I have the other one of those," he said, remembering the way he'd held it all the way home.

She flushed, a smile flitting around her lips. "You need soup, Steve. Someone to take care of you."

Great, Steve thought disgustedly. Whatever he'd been missing in his life was standing at the foot of his bed, looking at him with all the desire and heat of someone who'd just found a stranded kitten and meant to give it a bath.

Speaking of which, four days was a bit much. While she trounced off into the kitchen to dish out some soup, he ducked into the bathroom for a quick shower.

Stepping out of the steam to the sound of a toaster popping, Steve examined the state of his beard. No time to shave now. Wrapping a towel around him, he walked into the bedroom as Cally entered with a tray. A bowl of steaming soup, three pieces of toast, and some fluffy scrambled eggs sent up a delicious aroma.

"All bland, all hearty and filling," she said. "You need your protein—"

She stopped in midsentence. He tucked in the towel at his waist. A drop of water wound its way from a spike of wet hair, down his neck, and across his chest. He'd have wiped it, but the towel was otherwise occupied.

"Don't you think you should be in bed?" she whispered.

He didn't argue, although the pounding spray *had* given him more energy. Padding over to the bed, he got in. With a wriggle, he brought forth the towel, ruffling his hair one more time. "I never wear anything in bed anyway. The sweats were for the chills."

"I see."

Cally kept her eyes on the platter of food. Bowl. Spoon. Plate. Fork. Glass of orange juice. The only things she could concentrate on. Maybe this way she could put one foot in front of the other and make it over to the bed.

Steve sat up eagerly as she approached, the sheet in a pool in his lap as he leaned forward. She clutched the edges of the tray until her knuckles turned white.

"I feel better already. The shower was refreshing."

"Mmm."

"You're a miracle worker."

The miracle would be setting this tray on his knees while keeping her gaze off his lap.

He smiled up at her looking not quite as pale, smelling fresh and soapy. His hair was wet, mussed by the towel, combed with his fingers, and slicked back by the palm of his hand.

"Have a seat." He bit into a piece of toast and nodded toward a chair.

Cally pulled up a black director's chair and folded her hands on her knees. "You should be careful." They should both be. "Having wet hair, I mean."

"Want to get the dryer and blow it dry for me?"

"No." Touching him was the last thing she planned on doing.

She was there out of friendship. All the old reasons remained why they shouldn't go any further. The fact that she wanted to, meant she hadn't gotten over her old ways of approaching relationships. It might also have something to do with the world's best specimen of the male chest sitting three feet away.

She looked at the abstract oil paintings on the walls, surprisingly soothing flashes of pure color. She looked at the quilt picking up the same colors. She looked at everything but Steve Rousseau.

Simple, really. She'd hover like a hen, make jokes, keep his mind occupied with chatter about the office. They could even play a couple hands of gin rummy. She suspected he'd be a poor loser. Or a ruthless winner. Would he be as ruthless in bed?

"Ahh." He lay back with a sigh, an arm cocked over his head. The hair under his arms was black, still damp, as curly as the hair flaring out over his chest. "Your soup was marvelous. The entire meal was."

"You need your strength."

"Who needs strength to lie around in bed?" His mouth was crooked into a smile. The most deadly, dangerous, inviting smile she'd ever seen. It didn't help to remember it was the only thing he was wearing.

Her cheeks flamed with a rising heat. "How's the fever?"

"Down, I think. The aspirin was a good idea."

"Anything's better than your home remedies. I can't believe you were using weights." She scowled toward the weight set in the far corner of the room.

"I thought I could sweat it out Sunday night."

"Men! Blankets, fruit juice, and some much-needed food are what this doctor calls for. And rest." Yes, rest. She pounced on the idea. As soon as she stopped fluffing pillows, straightening blankets, and got rid of that tray, she'd be out of there. "I've got to let you get some sleep."

"I've been doing nothing but sleeping. And dying." And thinking of you.

During the empty days he'd thought about little else. Such as what if he played "let's pretend" too long and never got the chance to tell her how he really felt?

This time when she came back from the bathroom with his glass of water and another aspirin, he wouldn't be fool enough to miss the opportunity. When she handed him the glass, he touched her wrist. She flinched but tried to hide it. "How late are you staying?"

Cally felt the tremors of electricity up and down her arm. As long as you need me, she wanted to say. His eyes were more intense than any fever could cause. She touched his forehead, admitting only to herself how much she'd wanted to. It was warm, but not alarmingly so. Unlike the heat in her own cheeks, the crazy hammer of her heart, the conga beat of blood in her veins where his fingers pressed her pulse.

"I know I'm in no shape to ask you this," he said.

"Then don't ask."

Her voice was breathy. Lord, she was lovely.

"You could stay." There, he'd offered. He couldn't push.

He watched her throat move as she swallowed. So pale. Her skin was soft, warm, shadowed by curtains of dark hair waving around it. It put him in mind of making love in the dark.

"Steve—"

He interrupted her before she could turn him down. "Considering the condition I'm in, I've never offered a woman less, but I'm offering just the same. Stay the night."

He kissed her wrist. He kissed the inner part of her forearm. When he kissed the soft spot inside her elbow, her knees almost buckled.

"You promised no kisses," she said.

"Not on the mouth," he amended. "Read the fine print." His teeth made tiny bites on her skin. "Anyway, I wouldn't want you to catch this flu."

He was going to have to catch *her* if he didn't stop. Her legs were as shaky as her resolve. His mouth was climbing her arm, his lips skimming back down. The hairs on her neck tingled. Her own lips were wet, moist, but ignored for the attention he paid her fingertips. He turned her hand over, and his tongue pressed into the center of her palm.

"Stay."

One word.

Her reply could be equally brief, if only she knew what it should be.

"I, I didn't bring anything to wear."

Even Cally rolled her eyes at that one, curling her palm into an irritated fist, regretting to her toes the way it made Steve smile. He was getting to her and he knew it. He wouldn't back off now. Ruthless. The word made her shudder deep inside.

"You don't have to wear anything. However, I do have a pair of silk pajamas."

"I knew you would!"

He raised his brows in pleased acknowledgment. "Were you imagining me in bed?"

"No, I just—never mind." She was babbling. She was ready to say yes and ready to run and trying desperately to remember Dr. Curtis's emergency after-hours number.

That's when the phone rang.

Steve reached for the sheet.

"Don't you dare," Cally said. "You stay in bed." Locating the ringing instrument, she carried the portable phone to the bed.

"Hi, Mom." Steve sighed. "Radar," he said to Cally, "the woman is infallible. Yes, Mom," he continued into the receiver, "I'm fine. How did you know I was sick? . . . The worst of it is over. . . . Aspirin, toast, and soup. Cream of potato. . . . No, not from a can. Cally made it and brought it over. She's taking good care of me." He'd reached for her hand again, bringing it to his chest, pressing the back of it to his heated skin.

Despite the whirling in her veins, Cally noticed

he didn't explain her to his mother. Had he mentioned her already?

"And some eggs, scrambled, for protein. That's what she said."

Cally slipped her hand out of his.

"Rest? Mom, I've been doing nothing but resting. It's only been a week. It's nothing, honest, I'm much better." And he'd prove it, if Cally would get back in there.

But she was rinsing dishes in the sink, getting ready to leave, he could feel it. He put his hand over the receiver and called her name. She didn't answer. Steve cursed silently but vehemently. He couldn't very well chase her across the apartment, buck naked, carrying a portable telephone while his mother dictated a recipe for her own cream-of-potato soup.

When he heard the foyer closet open, he put his palm over the receiver again. "Cally, wait!"

She leaned around the bedroom door, shrugging into her coat. "Time for you to go to sleep. I'll see you in a few days."

"Wait! What? . . . No, Mom, I got that part. Oregano."

"Sleep tight." Cally winked from the doorway.

Damn her, she was enjoying this. She knew he was helpless, and so did he. "Take a cab," he shouted. "Mike will call you one from the lobby. It's too late for the subway. What, Mom?. . . . No, I was just saying good-night to Cally."

"Well, tell her to take a cab. It's too late for the subway," his mother said.

"I know, Mom. I know." It was way past too late. The next time he saw Cally, he was going to let her know that in no uncertain terms.

Seven

"Cally," he growled into the phone.

"You're not asleep yet?"

"I wanted to make sure you got home all right."

"Mike the lobby guard wouldn't let me step outside until the taxi arrived."

"I'll give him an even bigger check next Christmas."

"That's okay. I gave him a kiss on the cheek—that softened him right up."

"Funny, that never works for me."

She laughed, the vixen. She was out of touching range and saucy as all get-out. Steve, on the other hand, was stewing. He'd gotten them both worked up to a fever pitch that exceeded anything he'd suffered in the last week. If he'd blown the just-friends act, he'd blame it on delirium. But first, he had to make sure she was coming back.

Slouching down in bed, the sheet was his only covering. He'd kicked everything else off. He pictured Cally in her own bed, absentmindedly rubbing the inside of her arm.

"I think Mike got a better deal than I did. All I got was a handshake." One he still felt. Flu wasn't the only thing that could make a body ache. "When are you coming back?"

"You should be fine in a day or two," she said. "Do you really need me?"

Yes, he wanted to shout. He needed her. It surprised the heck out of him. He didn't just need someone to care for, but someone to let care about him. She'd brought him soup, humored him in his foulest mood, laughed, and made the whole place light.

And he loved her.

Suddenly faced with the fact that he wanted her in his life, in his apartment, Steve was going to deal with it. Head-on. Just as he dealt with everything else. "What are we going to do about this, Cally?"

He meant "us." Cally wasn't sure she was ready for an "us." "Take a couple aspirin and call me in the morning?"

He cursed, but not so she'd hear it. "I'm calling you right now."

"You should be sleeping."

"With you," he grumbled. Her responsiveness to his touch said one thing. Her skittishness another. But he wanted her. All week long, as he tried to keep her out of his mind, she'd returned to his thoughts, feverish, explicit thoughts and homey, comfortable thoughts. She'd made his impersonal white box a home. Ever since he'd opened the door to see her standing there, he'd known.

He sighed.

"Tired?" she asked.

"Yeah." His whole body was. He didn't want to play games anymore, flirting his way into her heart one small step at a time. "Come back," he said. Two plain words. Did they sound like the plea they were?

Her laughter drifted across the line. "Tonight? Hardly. You need your sleep more than you need me."

His gut twisted. Was it that easy for her to turn him down? Maybe she meant it. Except for their kisses, she'd kept him at arm's length all along.

"Tomorrow then," he said, gritting his teeth, bargaining for what he could get.

"You'll be fine."

Steve kicked the last of the coverlet off the bed. He didn't want her to let him down gently. He wanted rough, his beard sandpapering her skin, her delicate arms, the white of her inner thighs. He wanted her to ache for him the way he ached for her, to explode for him the way he longed to . . .

"I promise I won't kiss you good-night," he ground out.

"You agreed," she chided softly, "no kisses."

"I didn't kiss you on the mouth. It's not the same thing at all."

He could have fooled her. Cally could feel heat and soft abrasions up and down her arm from where he'd scraped her with his beard, loved her with his tongue. She found her hand curled into a loose fist over a palm that itched with sensation.

They both paused to lick their lips.

"I never promised not to kiss your neck," he said. "Or reach under your hair and run my mouth over your skin. Or your earlobe. Or your collarbone."

She rubbed a hand over the tense spots as he named the parts of her body, shivering at the sensations her imagination called to life.

"I don't recall any promises about kissing your breasts."

Cally swallowed so hard he must have heard it. "Steve."

"I want to see what's under that sweater. Do your nipples show through that white tank top? Are they hard now? How would it feel if my mouth were there?"

She didn't answer. She didn't have to. Her rapid breaths said it all.

"I could kiss them," he murmured, "suckling them like a man, not a baby. Would you like that?"

She was in bed. Light from the streetlight strewed shadows around the room, but they were nothing like the shadows she imagined there, of figures cast on the wall, two people moving in a rhythm as old as time, making one motion. Making love. "Steve, please."

"Please what? Kiss you again? Where? Tell me where you want me, Cally."

"I can't. Steve, don't, this is crazy."

"I'm only telling you what I'd do." His voice was gruff.

The silence stretched between them.

"It's a big bed, Cally. It's empty without you."

She dragged in a shuddering breath, entranced and mystified, her head still whirling. "What are you doing to me?"

"Nothing," he replied, teeth clenched, as reality set in. "How can I if you won't let me near you?"

"I can't, and you're sick."

"Sick of being alone." He meant that. She'd never know how much. "Will you come back?"

"When?"

One word. She'd stepped over the edge.

* * *

It had been a week since she'd stopped by Steve's apartment. She hadn't seen him; she'd only talked to him on the phone from her office. It was safer that way. Although after that late-night call she wasn't even sure of that. As with their first kiss, he never brought the subject up. How they could pretend to be just friends was successfully keeping her off balance. Helping him plan an ides-of-March party was keeping her busy.

"Will we have to wear togas?" she innocently asked.

"You'd like to see me wrapped in a sheet again, eh?"

Her cheeks flamed, and Cordelia gave her a weird glance as she dropped newspapers on her desk. "Uh, tell me more," Cally said as Steve finished outlining his plans. "Should I bring something?"

"Only your beautiful self."

"Funny. You must still be delirious from your fever."

Steve said nothing. They both remembered Thursday night well enough. He wanted more than a memory. He wanted a reenactment.

Cally quickly cleared her throat. "I'll get there at seven. That way I can help set things up."

"I've got a caterer. Some funky outfit from Tribeca. I think you'll like 'em."

He made it sound as if the whole thing was being designed to please her. She dismissed the thought.

"As long as you don't have a relapse—"

"Yes, Mom. I'll reheat the rest of the soup you dropped off Tuesday."

She'd left the crock with Mike the guard. It had been a cowardly move, but it had kept her from facing the butterfly brigade that set up shop in her stomach every time she thought of walking down that hallway and knocking on his door.

She hung up the phone, half crazy to call Dr. Curtis, but she was just back and booked for two weeks solid.

Cally needed to discuss the one, not-too-flattering thing she'd learned about herself in the last week: She'd been waiting for Steve Rousseau to mess up. She'd been too busy protecting herself, watching him for signs of thoughtlessness, temper, a host of bad habits.

Thursday night should have been the ultimate test. He was at his less than best, grumpy and sick and in no mood to put on a front. Wonder of wonders, she'd liked him better than ever. She'd trusted him. He'd let her care for him, and in a strange way she was grateful.

From friendship to caring, they'd crossed a line she hadn't even seen.

Elbows on her desk, Cally bowed her head and ran her hands through her hair with a sigh. Caring was okay, as long as she didn't mistake it for love. Love was where things went wrong, people got hurt. You could keep the people you cared for. But people you loved never stuck around long. That was one line she wouldn't cross again.

But what about this coming Saturday, after the party? They'd gotten so close, so intimate last time. Pictures of his shower-slick body invaded her dreams. This time he'd ask for more than just a good-night kiss. Was she ready?

Yes. She knew she wanted him. A deep, hidden part of her trembled every time she heard his voice. She was ready to give, she just didn't want to lose herself in the process.

"We're capable of an adult no-strings relationship," she muttered, unfolding a *Herald Tribune*. "Just so long as love doesn't enter into it." It was the only rule she had left.

"Hi," he said.

As if it were any other night.

As if she weren't completely aware of the fact that they could end this night as lovers.

So she said something brilliant, "Hi, yourself," and stood there on the threshold, clutching a bunch of blood red carnations she'd picked up from a street vendor. She'd gotten it wrong already; men were supposed to bring the flowers, weren't they?

"I didn't know if you'd have centerpieces," she explained.

"I thought you'd be the centerpiece of the evening." He grinned.

"Just don't lay me in the center of the table." Her mouth dropped open, the meaning of the double entendre hitting her like a double-barreled shotgun. "I can't believe I just said that."

Leaning against the doorframe, Steve laughed. "If that's fine with you, it's fine with me." His eyes were dark, sparkling, his mouth in a wry twist. "Welcome back," he said softly.

Her insides turned to Jello-O. So did her sparkling repartee. "Maybe I should put these in some water." She tried to step forward into the foyer. He didn't move. They ended up chest to chest,

Steve smiling as if he'd expected her to come to him all along.

"Aren't you going to say hello?"

She searched her mind. It must have been hiding wherever her voice had gone. "Didn't I?"

"Not properly."

He put his hands on her waist and took her in his arms. Slowly, so her nerves had time to set up a drumbeat of rhythm in her veins. Carefully, deliberately, to make sure neither of them missed the importance of it. Then he backed her up against the door and kissed her senseless.

Finally, after approximately a lifetime, Steve noticed where they were standing, the flowers crushed between them, the elevator dislodging its occupants. He took his tongue out of her mouth.

Cally was lost in his blue eyes. Vaguely, she touched the back of her hair where it had been flattened against the door. She licked her lips. No lipstick remained. She definitely wasn't ready for this. Carrying the flowers across her body like a shield, a Miss America whose crown was tipped most definitely askew, Cally strolled unsteadily into the foyer.

Steve followed, a grin on his face. "I went to the doctor Monday, did I tell you?"

She was being stalked. She had to get her nerves, her pulse, and everything else under control before she threw herself back in his arms. Besides, she had to find a vase for these flowers.

"I'm not contagious anymore," Steve elaborated, following her through the swinging doors into the kitchen.

The caterer glanced up in shock.

"Not that kind of contagious," Steve added. "Cally, meet Jeff."

The caterer nodded and immediately went back to work. He wore black Chairman Mao pajamas, an earring dangling to his collarbone, and a carrot-orange flattop haircut. Despite his feigned indifference, he backed subtly away as Steve pushed into the tiny alcove.

"Excuse me." Wending his way to the living room, Jeff tossed on a black overcoat that fluttered around his calves. "I'll be back at eight P.M. to pass things around. Before then, don't touch a thing. I've got it just perfect."

"Autocratic, isn't he?" Cally asked as the door slammed.

"Don't see why." Steve picked a cracker off a carefully arranged platter and dragged it through some pâté.

"Steve!"

"By eight-thirty no one will notice."

"*He* will. Do you own a vase by any chance?" she exclaimed in exasperation, crouching to peer into the back of a cupboard.

"You mean to put flowers in?"

"No, to save toenail clippings."

"Sure. I always save my toenail clippings." With that, he reached over her to retrieve a respectable enough vase from the cupboard over the refrigerator. "Will this do?"

Having oxygen pumped into the suddenly airless kitchen would have been even better, but Cally couldn't find the breath to mention it. Standing up in such a small space wasn't easy, not with Steve's body suddenly aligned with hers from knee to chest.

She slinked out of the body press, gaze fastened on the faucet as she filled the vase with water and began puttering with the flowers. "Got a knife?"

He handed her a paring knife, pressing his thigh softly to hers as he took up position beside her. "Want anything else?"

She wanted to know how much longer they'd be alone. If he kept that up, her resistance would be measured in seconds instead of hours.

She took her time trimming the stems, the paring knife snipping uncomfortably close to her thumb when Steve ran a hand appreciatively down her back. A Japanese flower arranger couldn't have been more concerned with placing the blossoms just so.

"How about—" Her voice was a dry screech. Vigorously, she cleared her throat. "How about a drink?"

"What'll you have?"

"Whatever you're having."

She glanced back over her shoulder. He was smiling, softly, dangerously. He had his glasses on, damn him. How could she concentrate when he looked like a little boy, a studious, concerned little boy who'd just caught the world's most precious butterfly and wanted to study it awhile longer.

Before picking the wings off it.

"I'm not drinking tonight," he said.

She pulled her mind back to the conversation.

"I lost ten pounds to the flu, despite some marvelous home cooking. I think alcohol would knock me out." He ran the tips of his fingers down her spine. "And I want very much to stay awake."

"Ten pounds? Wow." She had a master's degree in political science? Duh, wow. You'd think she could come up with better rejoinders. Even under extreme provocation.

Such as his breathing down her neck when he bent to whisper in her ear.

"My ribs practically stick out in the shower."

She closed her eyes tightly. She didn't want to think of what else stuck out in the shower. She was quivering like the Jell-O salad with the marshmallows in it.

"Jell-O salad?"

"Pardon me?" Steve straightened.

"You hired a caterer for *this*?" She waved an arm, taking in the platters of crackers with processed cheese and olives, the rolled-up pimento bologna speared with toothpicks. There were peanut-butter-and-jelly sandwiches, cut into quarters, cocktail franks to be heated over cans of Sterno, and for dessert, rice-cereal treats.

"He calls it retro cuisine," Steve explained.

"And what are we drinking, grape Kool Aid?"

Just then the caterer hustled back in, a platter of meatballs held high.

Cally had to admit, they smelled wonderful. Her mouth was watering, and for the first time that night it had nothing to do with Steve Rousseau. "What is this?"

"Made with cream-of-mushroom soup, darling, and please step back." With a flourish, Jeff lit the first can of Sterno.

The doorbell rang. Steve glared at the caterer, who'd taken over their space, and forced a smile. "The guests are here."

She wouldn't sigh. Neither would she laugh from sheer relief. Instead, her gaze held Steve's for a long moment. "You'd better show them in."

The party went well. Steve had chosen a comfortable mix of people, most of them coworkers

Cally had met previously. Most were married, all were having a good time.

Except the host and hostess.

The "just friends" routine clearly wasn't working. In fact, it was misfiring as badly as an old car. Every time Cally tried to sweep past Steve, he found a reason to block her path. It wasn't subtle, once or twice it was downright clumsy, but he wanted to touch her, if only in passing. He wanted to catch that look in her wide blue eyes; cautious, but not running. Was she ready? Was he? Would he be doing her harm by rushing her into anything?

For the first time since he'd met her, he actually wanted to call Dr. Curtis for advice. For the first time in his life, he was having second thoughts.

But it wasn't surprising. For the first time in his life, he was in love.

Cally chatted. She mingled. She milled. As long as she stayed away from Steve she was okay. But each time she came near, radar seemed to veer her into his path. Every time she escaped his intense gaze, it was with pounding heart and sweaty palms. She could barely hold on to the tray.

"You're here to enjoy the party, not serve it," Steve scolded.

When his breath brushed her ear, her wrists became as weak as her knees. The tray dipped. His hand was instantly on her inner arm, a casual touch that made her recall Thursday night. When he let go, every other part of her remained on alert. It was exhausting.

It was also obvious she wasn't just a date anymore. She'd seen a couple of women eyeing Steve, glancing at her, then giving up.

"I am not marked property!" she wanted to yell. Not that it would do any good. Steve was convinced she was going to be his. And no matter how she wanted to argue with that assumption, she lacked the words, the backbone, and the desire to make it stick.

If only these people were strangers, she could slink off into a corner and hide. She mingled some more, picking up bits and pieces of conversation.

"The Stealth bomber. Invisible, right? So how come I'm seeing pictures of it in the papers? And on TV?"

"The ides of March? What exactly are we celebrating? The toppling of dictators? Maybe Steverino's going for the top spot at AmeriConGroup. That'd keep him busy."

"Ask Cally. You planned this party with him, didn't you?"

"Not really. Steve seemed to have everything set."

"Oh."

Finally she couldn't avoid stopping by the group of men who'd gathered around Steve.

"You didn't invite Randy?" one of them asked.

"I couldn't get in touch with him," Steve replied. "But I saw his partner Cooper at the gym and told him to tell Randy."

There was a groan all around. "You didn't invite Cooper, did you?"

"Of course not."

"Good, I was ready to get my coat."

It was obvious no one liked Cooper.

"Excuse me," Cally interrupted. "You mean, you asked Cooper to invite Randy to your party, then you didn't invite Cooper?"

"Say that again?"

McIntyre of the legal department interjected, "I think what she's trying to say, Steve, is that you asked the party of the first part to ask the party of the second part to a party the party of the first part wasn't invited to. Isn't that correct?"

"Lawyers make everything easy, don't they?" Steve retorted.

Everyone laughed.

Cally frowned. "Emily Post would roll over on her chaise longue, and Miss Manners would carve you up for breakfast."

Steve lowered his voice, and his glance. "She's not the woman I'd most want to see at breakfast anyway." His meaningful look wasn't missed by the men surrounding them. Appreciative oohs and aahs filled the air, even a gruff "Go for it, Stevie."

Normally Cally would have had a retort tailor-made to set Steve Rousseau back on his heels. Instead she was mortified to find herself blushing, hemming and hawing, and generally flubbing it. "I'm—I'm going to see to the canapés."

She stalked away, head high, color higher, followed by another round of chuckles.

"You're acting like a virgin!" she told herself, storming into the kitchen.

"I beg your pardon?" Affronted, Jeff swept his fingertips over his brush cut.

Cally stopped dead. "Uh, talking to someone else."

He looked over her shoulder, saw nothing but the flapping white saloon doors behind her, and cocked a brow. "Oh," he said, as if that summed up his opinion of the matter.

"Cally, do we have any more white wine?"

Steve was smiling at her across the counter

dividing the kitchen from the living room. Wasn't there any place in this apartment where someone could go for privacy? There was always the bedroom, a small voice reminded her. She didn't want to think about it.

"I have no idea about the state of your liquor cabinet. I'm not your wife, you know."

"So I should stop treating you like one? You didn't have to serve hors d'oeuvres, you know."

She ignored him. At least the search for wine kept her back to him while she combed the pantry beside the stove. Thoroughly.

She turned around with a satisfied, "Whew! No wine," and bumped right into his chest.

He backed her against the counter, the edge angling into her hips. "If I treated you like a wife, you'd think it was the greatest honor a woman ever received." Thigh to thigh, his pelvis pressed hers.

Cally's eyes flashed. "That is the most old-fashioned, chauvinistic, Neanderthal remark! Next thing you know, you're going to be telling me motherhood is the be-all and end-all of my existence."

In the close confines of the kitchen he laid a hand flat on her abdomen, pressing it between them with his body. "It would be something, wouldn't it, Cally? You and me, and a baby inside you."

Suddenly it wasn't the activity or the embarrassment making her cheeks red and her knees weak. The slight, insistent pressure of his hand had her quaking inside. Fear, need, and desire were an overwhelming combination.

"Hmmph!" the caterer said. "If you could bear to excuse me for a moment, I'd like to pass."

It wasn't enough that they break apart. The kitchen was so narrow, they had to retreat to opposite sides of the room to let the man by.

"Thanks so very much," Jeff purred, raising a tray high over his head. The doors flapped shut behind him like wagging tongues.

Eight

" 'Windows,' 'men,' and 'cigarettes'!"

Cally frowned and drew faster.

" 'View,' 'men,' Maybe it's 'human'—*Of Human Bondage!*"

" 'Bondage'? Oh, this should be fun. *Women in Chains!*"

"The first word is one syllable!"

"Then it's not 'window,' is it?"

" 'See men smoke.' 'Seamen' . . .? 'Semen'?"

" 'Glass'!"

Cally nodded thankfully toward Steve. Glass. The material her nerves were made of.

The guests had dwindled to six. The pad of paper they were using for Pictionary was down to its last three sheets. Now if only she could draw a convincing "er-ie," she'd be done. The window glass, the symbol for man, and the cigarette ash weren't getting her far.

Then Steve shouted it out. " 'Glass Men-ash-erie.' *The Glass Menagerie!*"

She could have thrown her arms around his

neck. She handed him the crayon in surrender. "I told you I'm no good at this."

"Made perfect sense to me." So did the quick but definite kiss he placed on her lips before he let her sink into the sofa.

As he picked his movie title from the bowl, Cally glanced at the other couples. Three of them. All married. It was past one. No one had offered her a ride home. Why should they? They expected she'd stay.

So did Steve.

So did she.

Unfortunately, Pictionary wasn't a game for long silences. She had to shout something out. Looking at the multiple rings on the board, she thought of a dozen donuts. *"The Dirty Dozen!"*

Steve stared at her in astonishment. "That's it."

Everyone looked at her, then at Steve. Groans. "You two had that planned."

"Fix!"

"She guessed it, honest."

"Yeah, right."

"Game's over." Joe and Natalie rose, laughing and shaking their heads.

"One more," Cally suggested.

"Only if it's *Two for the Road.*"

"Or *Coming Home.*"

The guests milled in the doorway to the bedroom. Cally helped picked coats off the bed, lagging behind as Steve saw his friends to the door.

She watched him. His glasses still on, he looked festive but casual in a multicolored V-neck sweater, mostly navy shot with pink confetti. It didn't exactly rival Jeff the caterer's fashion statement, but it was different enough to be a touch rebellious. His form-fitting jeans were comfortably worn, a pocket frayed. His hair was slightly mussed from running his hand through it while fighting for the right guess in their game of charades.

More than once this evening she'd glimpsed him running a hand through his hair in frustration as she'd sidestepped his passes. Was he as nervous as she?

Why should either of them be nervous? Steve was a good friend, a willing ear, an easy companion who appreciated and set off her sense of humor. He wasn't just everything a woman could want in looks, she was sure he was everything a woman could want in a lover.

So why was she worried? Tingling? Plain scared? "It's your choice, Cally," Martha Curtis would say. "You're free to choose." And of all the men she'd ever met, Steve was the one she'd choose. That didn't mean he thought the same of her. She thought of Dr. Curtis again: "You're responsible for your own choices, you can't make them for someone else."

Great. That meant she had to put herself on the line emotionally, sans the wishful thinking that had clouded her other relationships. Jump off a cliff and wait to be caught.

"I will not insist he love me. I'm a grown woman. We can have a relationship, even an affair. That doesn't mean I have to hurl myself into this or pin everything on what he thinks."

She turned down the quilt, briskly running a hand over it, smoothing what had been disarranged by coats and purses. This wasn't self-protection. It was about giving. Sharing. Steve wanted her; what was more, he needed her. She'd sensed it that night she'd brought him soup, tenderness, company. And she wanted to give him that.

She sat heavily on the edge of the bed. But love-making meant love. Cally knew that. And she knew she was teetering on the edge of loving him. If only she could avoid that, she stood a chance of avoiding the mistakes that invariably accompanied it. Her only safety net was that Steve never had to know.

He walked in, wrapping his arms around her from behind. "Thanks for turning down the bed," he said softly. For turning him inside out, he might have added.

She ran a hand over his arm.

"Do you want me to stay?" Her voice faltered, not her resolve.

His breath released in a long sigh. "Please?"

She nodded, turning and looking into his eyes. She had her heels on; he'd slipped his shoes off a couple hours ago. They weren't eye to eye, but they were closer. Without letting go, he danced her over to the nightstand and set his glasses down.

"Have I ever told you I like those glasses?" she asked, a smile belying her fears.

"What I have in mind might be a bit rough and tumble for glasses."

"Ah." Teasing. She could deal with teasing. "Is this the Rousseau of 'noble savage' fame?"

"That was another Rousseau," he growled, his mouth playing over hers. Tickling. Licking. Prodding. She might be right, savage would be good, so would slow—so would anything, as long as he was certain this was right for both of them. "You sure you want this, Cally?"

Her mouth was on his jaw. He felt the pulse

pounding against the bone, her tongue slipping out to trace it. "I want to make you happy," she whispered.

"What about you?"

"That would make me happy too."

"Is that enough?"

She drew back, taking his face in her hands, aware his arms were locked around her. Except for the kiss, he'd taken no liberties at all. She inhaled, felt her breasts expanding against his chest as she did so, and stopped. She did it again, luxuriating in the way it felt. "For tonight, yes."

"I want it to be good for you too."

"I don't see how it could be bad."

Steve's pulse raced. No woman should look at a man the way she was looking at him without a bed nearby. But if she kept touching him, they'd never make it that far.

The material of her dress bunched beneath his hands. "I like this dress, did I say so?"

She shook her head and pouted. "Not a word."

"You're right. I should have sent you home to change."

"What?" She tried to be huffy, to stiffen in his arms. It didn't work.

"Too many buttons." He frowned in a transparent attempt at disapproval. He ran his fingers up her back, following a path of pearl buttons. The trail started at her hips and rose to a wide V, baring her shoulders. From there he traced black angora around her shoulders, one finger on her skin, one on the soft wool. "I don't suppose I could simply pull this off?"

"You'd stretch it." Her body shuddered like her voice, thinking of soft things stretching. From the darkness in his eyes she knew he was thinking along the same lines.

"The buttons definitely have to go," he stated hoarsely. "Turn around."

Her heart skipped a beat. This was it. But the lights were still on in the living room, here in the bedroom. Music played somewhere. Dishes were piled on the counter. She might be ready, but that didn't mean she was relaxed.

Except when he held her, and he wasn't anymore. With his hands on her waist, he turned her away from him. One by one, he gently undid the buttons. The dress slid down her shoulders. She crossed her hands over her breasts to hold it up.

"Cally." Her name was like a prayer on his lips. His hands stroked her sides, her thighs. The fabric clung, slipped, stretched taut until she released it. It fell.

"Steve?" She turned.

He was there, smiling, a faraway look in his eyes. The slip was cream satin, like the skin beneath it but cooler to the touch. With the lamp behind her, her hair was black, her face in shadow. The backs of his fingers caught on the satin, making a rasping sound, like her breath.

"Want to do the same to me?" he asked with a smile. "I'm getting ahead here."

There was a pun in there somewhere, Cally thought, tugging at the hem of the sweater he wore, pulling it over his head as he bent at the waist, his arms extended. The shirt would have to come next. Her nerve would have to last. But there were so many buttons, and he insisted on standing so close, his hips pressed forward, teasingly brushing her abdomen, occasionally pushing, brazenly advertising. She would not back up.

"You're not making this easy," she scolded.

"Easy is no fun."

"And playing hard to get is?" Was that it? Would he lose interest when she stopped saying no? Cally flubbed the third button for the third time and tried stalking off.

"Hold on a minute." He gripped her arm loosely.

"What."

"That's enough." He impatiently pulled the shirt out of his waistband and tugged it over his head, turning it inside out in the process. He flung it on the floor.

Cally went after it. She had to run somewhere. "You'll ruin your shirts doing that."

"Never had brothers, did you? All men's clothes are made to lie on the floor between washings. Don't believe me?" He tossed his T-shirt in the same corner. "You should have asked Bill tonight, he owns a laundry."

"Right. I would have said, 'Uh, excuse me, Bill, but can Steve throw his clothes on the floor? We've been having an argument about that.' "

"Is that what we're having?" he asked softly. "An argument?"

He was behind her again. Every tiny hair on Cally's neck was at stark attention. The slip couldn't hide the goose bumps, the quivering. All the willpower in the world, which she seemed to have lost somewhere along the way, couldn't hide the emotions tumbling through her.

"It's not a question you come right out and ask at a party," she said, stalling.

"No? I asked him what harm it would do angora if I stripped that dress off you."

She whirled. "You what!"

Fool, her heart cried out. He'd been teasing.

Now he was standing there smiling, thumb hooked in the waistband of his jeans, looking for all the world like some disreputable cowboy eyeing the most beautiful dance-hall girl in the world. He sucked in the corner of his mouth, as if tasting dust from a long cattle drive, as if looking at her made his mouth water.

"Are you going to come over here, or are we going to talk all night?"

Her arms were still crossed over her front, the chills prodding her nipples to unmistakable peaks.

The caveman facade faltered. He knew she had a dozen reasons to be hesitant. Justifiable reasons. For some crazy reason, the fact that he hadn't been able to ease those fears hurt. "Cally, you have to come of your own accord. Otherwise, we'll call it a night."

She didn't speak. Feeling his gut tighten, his smile do the same, he walked over to where she was standing, bent, and picked up his shirt.

When he straightened, she reached out. Her hand glided over his bare chest. "I'm sorry," she whispered.

"No problem." He meant that. His own desire had blinded him, and he'd put them both in an uncomfortable, embarrassing position. He pulled the shirt roughly over his head, getting one arm in a sleeve, fussing to find the other.

"Here." She laughed, unbuttoning a button to make it easier for him. Then another. His head popped through the opening, his arm filling the second sleeve. Five buttons were undone. Chest hair peeked through a gap revealing a nipple. Cally drew her fingernails down the opening, pausing at the sixth button, his abdomen quivering at her touch.

He wrapped a hand around her wrist. "Why do I feel as if I'm the one coming undone here?"

She flicked open the last two buttons, running an open palm up his bared chest. Her gaze didn't follow. She couldn't meet his eyes until she'd said what she had to say. "I'm nervous. I don't want to make another mistake." *I don't want to mess up and fall in love, and I'm afraid I already am.*

He took her shoulders in his hands. "If you're not ready—"

"I am." She looked at him, steady, braver now. As long as she was touching him she knew it was right.

With one reach he flicked off the overhead light and kicked the door shut, leaving them in the soft light of the bedside lamp.

In three steps, four—who was counting?—they were standing beside the bed. "Okay?" he asked.

She wrapped him in a hug, her cheek pressed over his heart. "Just stay near me."

He laughed, the sound rumbling around in his ribs. "What I have in mind requires it."

She laughed then, too, and he eased her down.

The bed was huge. It could have been a cot. Except for when he reached into the drawer under the nightstand, they were never separated. Mouths sealed, arms entwined, legs atangle, he pulled her slip up, pausing over the two strips of satin joined by a center panel of lace that some lingerie shop dared sell as clothing. Dark hair showed through, tantalizing, springy, a lattice-work of lace easily pierced by a finger, or two.

She moaned, he listened, lingered. Then his

mouth came down on her in a kiss that had her arching in shock, gasping with stunned desire.

His second kiss was shockingly intimate, insistent, straight to the point.

Her body sang like a wire in the wind, vibrating and tautly strung. He was concentrating on one part of her body, but others were achy, needy. She touched them herself or led his hands there. The satin bunched over her breasts. The slope of her abdomen shimmied when a lock of his hair swept it. She wove her fingers through his hair, lifting his head, softly tugging him toward her. "I thought you were sick."

"I recover quickly." He covered her hand with his and lifting himself along her body, showed her where he wanted her to touch him. He groaned when she did so, but it was the price he had to pay if he was going to kiss her full on the mouth.

She felt the moisture on his lips, on her, the taste of honey. She quivered, clenching her hand around him. If he didn't stop that, she'd beg. But it was Steve who pleaded, a low growl in his throat as her hand imitated the motion they both needed.

Names were panted, moaned, whispered. The last shreds of clothing discarded somewhere inside the sheets. Mouths joined, hands explored, legs petted legs, twining, then opening.

"Put this on me," he requested.

She glanced at the packet clenched in his fingers.

"It may be your last chance," he said, inching away from where he was touching her, every nerve ending pounding for release.

Cally tore the cellophane with her teeth. Steve

groaned. He could feel those teeth as if they were scraping his skin. "Could you go a little faster?"

Cally made a knowing pout. "You're stepping on my lines."

"Not now, Cally."

"Having a little problem with self-control?"

"If you don't put that thing on me—"

"Okay." With that she touched him. The tip alone made him feel like a rocket before blast-off. Then the shaft, her fingers making soft circles, slow lines. "Done?" she asked softly.

"Baby, we've hardly begun."

With that he found her, opened her, and descended into a special hell of his own making called self-control.

He didn't have to ask her what she liked. She tightened around him, the sure slinky motion of her hips matched to the movement of his, abrading him, speeding him up, slowing him down. Nothing she did could lessen his desire, each motion leading to an inexorable increase, a building volcano.

He'd once seen a manhole cover blow off a vent in midtown Manhattan, spewing a stream of steam into the air. He knew just how it felt.

So would Cally. Then the earthquake hit. She cried his name, mewed it, demanded that he do what he was doing again and again.

Shuddering sensations flowed from one to the other, subsiding like the force of a wave at the sea's edge.

"Are you all right?"

Fifteen minutes might have passed. Thirty.

Steve dragged his fingers through her hair, combing it lazily as she laid her head on his chest.

"Fine," she murmured.

"Sorry I couldn't last longer."

"Steve . . ." she chided gently.

"It's supposed to last all night the first time. That's what it said in the manual, anyway."

She chuckled, listening to the precious sound of his own laughter as her ear pressed against his chest.

"You didn't—" he began.

"Simultaneous orgasms are a myth. It says that in the manual too." His chest was so smooth, the hair so crinkly, wiry and black. She straightened one with her finger, watched it spring back.

"You must have a different edition," Steve was saying. "Mine says there's no reason it can't be simultaneous every time."

"And earth shattering."

"And utterly overwhelming."

"Ahh. Well, I think you managed that part."

"Thank you very much."

"You're welcome."

"We could give it another try."

"I'm too tired to move, and you aren't going anywhere either."

He conceded. She'd let him get up once for a quick trip to the bathroom. Aside from that, she wasn't relinquishing her spot on his chest. She liked the sound of his voice from this vantage point. She blew out a breath and watched his nipple tighten.

"You were wonderful," he said. "Have I told you that less than a hundred times tonight?"

"You're up to ninety-six, I think."

"Can we manage four more?"

Cally cautiously raised her head and looked into his sparkling eyes. "You don't literally mean four more times—"

"Would you like to try three?"

"I'd like to try walking afterward. Besides, I like this part too." She was reveling in the feeling of rightness that pervaded her senses, having for once made the right choice, at the right time, with the right man. The future could wait. "Tell me things."

"Like what?" Like how much he loved her? Like how many women he'd had and how absurdly grateful he felt to her for—for what? For loving him back? She hadn't said so yet.

Neither had he, Steve realized with a guilty twinge. Once again he wasn't sure how to proceed. Would he scare her away? Or was that exactly what she was waiting for?

"Tell me about all your former girlfriends," she said.

"You want to hear about them now?"

"I'm feeling cocky."

"That should be my line."

"I mean, mister, that I could be compared to just about any woman in the world right now and come out on top. I'm feeling very secure."

"Well, in that case. You, my love, are better than any woman in the world, in my experience."

"Thank you."

"Anytime." He bent to kiss her forehead. "You know, I like the idea of your being on top."

"Who'd have guessed you were at death's door ten days ago."

"But then you were at my door. That's all I needed."

They lay quietly for a while.

"Will you tell me?" she asked softly.

"About the other women?"

Maybe she was pushing her luck. Maybe she should close her eyes and pretend there was no future, no past.

"There was only one long-term relationship. Tawny. And she was as glamorous as her name. A stewardess."

"You're kidding."

"And you're prejudiced. They're not all bimbos. She was very intelligent."

"And?"

"And I didn't appreciate her. I thought her constant travel would mesh well with my desire for work."

"And?"

"Relentless, aren't you?"

"I want to know." *I want to be prepared if anything goes wrong.*

"She left me once because I didn't make time for her. I wanted to show her what a mistake she was making, what a big shot I was going to be. So I proved her right by spending even more nights at the office. That's how I got to be the successful businessman I am today."

"Was this her apartment?"

"Mine. The one I got afterward."

"It doesn't seem like you."

"Let's say I don't long for its comforts while I'm at the office. The decor is strictly store-bought."

"And your personal life?" She yawned. It was getting harder to hold on to the string of this conversation. The evening had been exhausting, emotionally and physically, and there were still things neither of them had said.

Steve was breathing evenly, his chest rising and falling beneath her cheek.

"My personal life," he said slowly, testing the words, "has come alive since I've met you. I don't plan on making the same mistakes again, Cally. I want that promotion, but not at the cost of my life. You're part of that life now."

There. He'd said it. She wasn't clutching at his chest in fright, nor flinging off the sheets and marching out. She was staying right where she was. Fast asleep.

"Good-night, love," he whispered.

She was a burrower. He was a rover. When he awoke, he was on the far side of the king-size bed, his arms over his head, his legs spread. He had the disturbing idea he'd been snoring. Cally, meanwhile, was the bump under the covers in the middle of the bed. At least he hoped that was her. He prodded it gently with his knee. "Cally?"

A mumbled don't-wake-me-whoever-you-are moan came from under the layers of bedding.

"Cally."

A hand poked out, slapping the mattress as if the alarm clock were there.

His chuckle was deep, shuddering through the mattress springs.

The hand stopped.

Cally knew what she looked like in the morning. No way did she want Steve Rousseau to see her.

Permission to be yourself, she reminded herself. But that was in front of Dr. Curtis, not Steve.

A mangled head of hair inched out from under

the blanket. With an impatient swipe of her hand a face appeared from behind the dark curtain. "Morning?" She wasn't entirely sure.

"Eight A.M.," he said brightly.

"Ah." In that case she might find a dignified way of easing up beside him. She might not. Her hair needed a brush, her teeth needed a brush, and the crick in her neck was entirely his fault. She'd fallen asleep on his chest. It was romantic, but no way to sleep through a night.

"You kick in your sleep," she complained.

"You were seeking refuge?" He grinned at the pile of blankets. "Didn't know I was making love to gopher."

"Laugh all you want. You won't find it so funny when I insist on separate beds."

"Only if we can make love in both. Every night."

She searched for another wisecrack. He was, after all, laughing at every one of them. "Are you always so happy in the morning?"

"I'm usually a grump until I get my first cup of high octane."

"You wouldn't be smiling if you had your glasses on. I must be a mess."

"Do you always sleep that way? Like one of those bugs that curls up in a ball when touched? Come to think of it, you look a little like one of those bugs—"

The pillow hit him full force. "Not another word, Rousseau." She took the opportunity to scamper across him and into the bathroom before he could chase her.

"Oh, no!" she wailed. "This is even worse than *Les Misérables*."

"What?" he called from the other room.

"I look like something from *Cats*!" Or something one dragged in, she thought to herself. Her hair had been teased by pillows and hands into a mound. Her eyes were puffy from sleeping face-down, her cheek creased with a sheet's wrinkle. Reaching almost unconsciously for the tooth-brush, she found a new one, wrapped. He'd planned this. Yes and he'd been prepared the pre-vious night too.

Should she be mad? After all, she'd been sure to stuff a full complement of makeup and over-night toiletries in her purse. But that was in the other room.

She thought she heard his voice, dismissed it for the mumbling of a radio, and turned on the shower full blast. If she couldn't be attractive, at least she'd be clean.

Twenty minutes later she stepped back into the bedroom. Thank goodness he was one of those men who liked big fluffy towels. This one covered her from the knees up. He also had a robe slung across a chair for her. She put it on as he hung up the phone.

"Was that your mother?"

"I told her you were in the shower, so I said hi for you."

She gave him a drop-dead look. "I'm not even going to pretend— But that does remind me to call mine."

"Actually, I was ordering another bed."

Hint, hint. He was including her in his future.

She laughed. And the laughter never completely died away, even when he took her hand, tugged her toward him, and laid her back on the bed. Her hair was blown dry, still warm. He buried his face in it. They were gasping, groaning, and still laughing. Even when, especially when, she guided on the latex sheath. Not until the last minute, the last few seconds, when she gripped his arms in desperation, holding tight, pleading, did they both grow serious, close. He reached behind her to wrap his arms around her back, body to body, barely moving, but those moves, oh, Lord. She rocketed beneath him, shuddering and shaking, feeling his own body stiffen and jolt inside her.

Maybe the manual was wrong.

Nine

There was a knock on the door. "Stay right here," Steve whispered in her ear. He slid off her, picked up the robe, now lying discarded beside the bed, and tossed it around him. Despairing of finding the tie, he held it closed at the waist. He winked at her as he backed out of the room.

Cally sighed, shuddered, and missed him already. As long as he didn't back out of her life like that, she'd be fine, she thought. She forcefully shook her head, mangling her just-washed hair even more. She would not think discouraging thoughts. Nor would she get her hopes up.

Nor would she say "I love you" unless he absolutely dragged it out of her. He walked in with two white paper bags, a glass of orange juice, and a Sunday *Times*. Her heart tumbled like the two fat oranges that rolled off the edge of the tray and onto the bed.

"Where'd you get all this?"

"Deli delivery." He opened one bag and popped the plastic top off a cup of steaming coffee. "That's who I was calling." He winked.

Cally rummaged among the sheets for her satin slip. Lifting her arms overhead, she let it fall to her waist. "In my family we dress for breakfast," she said primly, belying the inner heat that hummed inside her when she caught his steady gaze. She knew from his look that he was seeing skin where now was satin, breasts where now was lace.

"I prefer al fresco," he replied.

"That means without walls, not without clothes," she corrected gently.

"Sometimes they're the same thing. Ways of covering up."

Just because they'd made love didn't mean she was ready to bare her soul to him. Neither was she keen on taking too much togetherness for granted. "Have to preserve some mystery," she said, carefully arranging herself on the bed so as not to jostle the tray. Taking a container of cream, she peeled it open with a fingernail and poured, concentrating on the cloudy swirls in her coffee.

Steve handed her a sugar packet. "Care to open this?"

She tore the corner with her teeth, only to find him watching her again.

"Not the first packet you've opened that way." He grinned. "Maybe I ought to keep you around to open all of them. Mustard, taco sauce, sweet and sour from the Chinese place—"

"Maybe you ought not to press your luck."

"You've got sugar on your lips." Before she could lick it off, he ducked his head, and his tongue met hers, gently picking off crystals of sugar.

"Sweet as ever," he said softly, making the blood flow in her veins like molasses, dark, sweet, and heavy.

Her fingers drifted over the corner of her mouth. "Was that all of it?"

"Mmm-hmm." He licked his own lips, tracing a wide, knowing smile. "I ordered some extra marmalade too."

"For coffee?" she asked.

He made a show of frowning. "For toast, maybe. There are other possibilities, if you want to be creative."

She wasn't so sure she did. Her stomach flip-flopped at the very idea of his licking anything else off her body. "I'd rather think of bagels," she replied, reaching into the second bag. At least her hands weren't shaking. Everything else seemed to be.

"Who'd have thought it," she said, filling up the silence with chatter. "I fall asleep in a strange man's bed and wake up a half-starved sex slave. Mama never said there'd be days like this."

Settling himself behind her, he balanced an elbow on one side of her and stretched his legs along the other. He planted a kiss on her bare arm, watching the goose bumps rise and fall. "Sorry I didn't make the breakfast myself, love."

Cally followed the bite of bagel with a gulp of steaming coffee. Why did he have to use the word *love* in that intimate, undeniable way? "If you can't stand the heat, order takeout, I always say."

Looking into his eyes, she knew the heat very well.

And Steve recognized the wall she built with wisecracks. She wasn't ready even to tease about a word like *love*. He swallowed a shot of disappointment with his coffee. Patience, he reminded himself.

Hefting an orange in his hand as if it were a softball, he said, "Try one. Fresh from Florida, or so they told me."

They shared one, peeling sections. When juice squirted on Steve's arm, he extended it to her. "It's your orange," he said, as if licking juice off a man's skin was something she did every morning.

But she complied. His intake of breath when her tongue touched him was the hiss of liquid on a hot surface. She returned to her breakfast with a saucy smile.

"Cally," he said flatly. Her name hung between them. He had to know. Too many things were being left unsaid. Until they were cleared out of the way, the morning would be tense. In fact, he could see months of tension ahead of them as he waited for her to catch up to his plans; the ones about the day she'd move in, the day they'd marry, how many children they'd have.

He chewed on a section of orange, appreciating the sharp tang. Patience and planning. It had worked so far. There were still barriers to be crossed, and they would be, one step at a time.

"Still seeing Dr. Curtis?"

She nodded, her lips pursed as she bit off a section of orange. He loved the way her mouth fit around it.

"How much longer?"

She shrugged, using a plastic knife to spread cream cheese on a bagel. "For however long it takes."

Dammit. She had to know he wanted her, and not necessarily with her doctor's permission. "Don't you think your bad choices in men are behind you?"

The answer was in her eyes. Yes. Cally knew if ever a man was going to be the one, it was Steve.

She felt his hand kneading her inner thigh, his fingers dancing under the whisper of satin.

"I want to be sure," she said, her gaze riveted on the tray. "I don't want to hurt either one of us by making the wrong decision. Or making it too fast," she added rapidly as he began to speak.

Steve sighed, glancing around the rumpled bed. She'd made a decision when she'd chosen to stay the night. He could have pointed that out to her, could have pointed out that she wasn't running away this morning, scooting out of his life with a lot of excuses. She was there. She was staying. How hard would it be to keep it that way?

But two could play at noncommittal. "We'll have to do this again sometime," he said.

"Mmm." She nodded, her mouth full. Wiping her fingers hurriedly on a napkin, she seized the newspaper, combing through the mound that was the Sunday *New York Times*. "Ever do a crossword puzzle together? It's fun with two."

Like a few other things he could think of. "We'll fight."

"No, we won't. Just remember I'm usually right. Now, where's a pen?"

Steve got off the bed and reached into the nightstand drawer. "You do them in pen?"

"Little-known secret, but when it comes to crossword puzzles, confidence is the name of the game."

That also applied to making promises for a lifetime. Before Steve could think of a way to fit that observation into the conversation, Cally was fluffing up a pillow at her back and raising her knees as a desk.

"You can't tell me you never make a mistake,"

Steve said, watching her fill in the first three words in black ink.

Cally smiled and blithely shook her head. "Not in crosswords."

He slid under the sheet and took up a place beside her, his arm draped over her shoulders "Whoa, you've already filled in a half dozen. Read me the clues."

"The overall theme is 'phobias.' But this clue is 'an Olympic symbol.' Five letters. *O-O-O-O-O*."

Steve groaned. "You've got to be kidding."

"It fits," she said with a superior tilt of her chin.

"So does *R-I-N-G-S*. What's seventeen down?"

"I do all the acrosses first, then the downs. The next clue is 'hoax.' A three-letter word."

" 'Con.' But what about seventeen down?"

Cally plucked an orange rind off her lap and grudgingly read seventeen down. " 'Cowboy roundup.' "

"Rodeo! 'Rings' is seventeen across. Told you so."

"Now the truth comes out! You're an 'I told you so'-er."

"Didn't I tell you so?" He nibbled on her shoulder. "Bara."

She shivered at the sensation, her handwriting taking a nasty tilt. "What?"

"Theda Bara, twenty-seven across."

"We have to do these in order. Here's one of the theme clues, 'fear of Greek assemblies.' "

"Agoraphobia," they said in unison.

"It usually means fear of open places."

"I know," he murmured, getting no visible response to running his hand down her back.

But a heart's pounding didn't show. Cally

sighed silently when he stopped. Perhaps now she could actually get the letters in the little boxes.

"Cally?" He ran a hand up her arm.

She inhaled sharply, blinked slowly, and looked over at him. "Yes?"

"Give me another theme question. One of the big ones."

She gave him a scathing glance. "That's getting ahead."

Again he ran his fingers down her arm. Anything to keep his mind on the puzzle, she decided. "Okay, 'fear of fuzzy sweaters.' "

"Wha—?" He chuckled, his abdomen rippling as he did so. Cally suddenly forgot anything having to do with words. The washboard of muscles tightened and he sat up straighter, scooting over to press his bare chest to her back. He tucked his chin on her shoulder, his voice soft in her ear. "*Angora*phobia."

She snorted. "You can't be serious." In a sense she hoped to heaven he was serious, about her. He was so eager to touch her, to be with her. So easy to argue with, easier to love.

"It's a pun and it fits. Write it down," he softly commanded, his mouth on her neck.

She wrote it in very very tiny letters.

"So that's how you get away with doing it in pen."

"No fair."

"Give me another then."

She searched out the big clues. "Okay, 'fear of agriculture.' "

"Agrophobia?"

She hated to admit it, it worked. "I think you've caught on to their method."

"There are a number of methods." He laved her

collarbone with his tongue. She dropped the paper in her lap. "No, don't stop," he said, hiding a grin behind her back. The previous night those had been her words. "Keep writing."

And he'd keep tormenting. He'd never examined a woman's back so completely. Her shoulder blades were smooth and easy to outline, her spine a subtle dip instead of a bumpy line. Her skin was soft. She smelled, mmm, wonderful. And tasted—

"Steve!"

Ah. He liked that arch. He ran his hand up it. The tactile survey ended with his hand sunk in her hair, grasping the nape of her neck, soothing with his fingers the tension he'd created there.

"Find a word you don't know?" he asked innocently.

He took the paper off her lap. Sometimes talk had to stop. Less often, time had to stop. As Steve slowly, suggestively fit the cap onto the pen and set it aside, his eyes held hers. With her hands free now, he lowered her to the bed. "Try a seven-letter word for you and me."

It was a long time coming, too many possibilities ran through her head, and counting their letters was impossible when he was touching her, kissing her deeply, pressing her legs apart with his, making her heart thunder and her pulse trip over some new discovery of tongue and hands.

" 'Ecstasy,' " she said with a moan when he thrust into her.

"I was thinking of 'now, love.' "

Now.

Love.

Cally could only think of another, simpler three-letter word. *Yes.*

"Bye, Mom." Steve hung up the phone, planting a kiss on the top of Cally's head as they lay side by side in the bed. It was almost one in the afternoon. "You should have said hello."

"Wearing this?" She laughed. His pajama bottoms fit in different places on her than they had on him. Her top half was as bare as that of a Tahitian native in a Gauguin painting. "I couldn't talk to your mother dressed like this."

"She wouldn't have known."

"Mothers always know."

He chuckled. With her ear against his chest, she loved listening. She'd also liked his brief weekly talk with his mother.

"You seem close."

"Since Dad died, I've tried to keep in touch. All of us do. You talk with your mother much?"

"Sure. I was just thinking I should call." And thinking of ways to avoid it. Her birthday was coming up. For so many years birthdays had meant calls from her father, always engineered by her mother. Although Cally had called a halt to the practice years ago, the memories remained.

"What's on TV?" she asked lazily, changing the subject.

"Leslie Howard in *Intermezzo.*"

Cally sighed. "I always had a crush on him."

"Trying to make me jealous?"

"He always had that faraway, romantic look because he was nearsighted. Did you know that?"

"Really."

She felt him stretch toward the end table. When

she glanced up, his glasses were perched on the end of his nose. "Like this?"

She couldn't have giggled harder if he'd put on a fake nose and glasses. Her breasts jiggled against his chest. How could he make her feel so at ease? Wasn't the morning after, now stretched into afternoon, supposed to be a self-conscious time?

He pulled the glasses even further down his nose, picked up a notepad and pen from the nightstand, and spoke with a guttural German accent. "Now tell me allll your prrroblems, *meine Liebchen.*"

"I don't have any problems," she said. Except that he'd just called her his love. Again.

"So all you needed vass de luff of a good man. Just as I suspected."

"That easy, huh?"

"No kidding." He set down the notepad and held her face in his hands. "I was the right man for you. I knew it from the beginning."

"The Prince Charming cure. Wait for the right man to come along, and all will be well. You're a romantic, you know that?"

"Dyed-in-the-wool."

"Then how come you always asked me to be an escort, not a date?"

"Uhhh, good question." He toed the edge of the entertainment section, surprised any of the paper remained on the bed after their lunchtime scuffle.

"Well?" She prodded him with a fingernail.

"To get you to go out with me. I thought that was obvious by now."

"It was."

Steve relaxed a hundred tense muscles. She wasn't storming out at his deception. "You knew?"

"All along."

"But you said you wouldn't date me."

"I pretended it wasn't really dating. As did you."

"But I was lying."

"And I was denying. The ways of love are never smooth." Love. It couldn't be this easy, could it?

"There was never anything wrong with you, nothing a psychoanalyst needed to cure."

She wished he were right. But the doubts remained. The men who'd left her couldn't all be wrong. And it hadn't always been their fault. There were times she'd been too quick to give up, even pushed them away, self-protecting to the end. "One can't be completely sure where other people are concerned."

"You can. I won't leave. I don't cheat. And I love you." He'd said it. And he could wait a week, a year, five minutes, to hear her say it back.

"Steve . . ."

"I'm not pushing. I know it takes time." It took thirty seconds of increasingly taut silence. She was cured. Hell, there was never anything wrong with her. Together they'd make it, if only she believed. "So what's the holdup?"

"Nothing."

"You're getting defensive."

"No, I'm not."

Damn. He released a harsh breath; the curse might have been said aloud. "Don't you see you don't have to doubt anymore? Self-confidence, remember? Trust me, believe in us."

"And we'll live happily ever after. You really think all problems can be solved with applied logic? One-minute decision making?"

"They have been so far."

"Your strategy worked, you got me in bed. Is that it?"

He didn't answer. Scrambling off the bed, she pulled the black angora dress over her head.

"Cally, wait."

She was picking a fight, running away. She didn't like the choice she was making. She'd promised herself honesty. She'd promised him honesty. "I—I don't believe, Steve. I don't trust being this happy. Maybe I should talk to Dr. Curtis."

"Doctors don't solve problems."

"No, they don't. But she's impartial, which is not at all how I feel about you."

"And how do you feel about me?"

The words hung there. Their gazes met. Cally's eyes were bright with something that made her blink. Steve ached to touch her, protect her. In bed he could show her, love her, heal her.

"I don't want to drag you into my problems, Steve."

He ran both hands through his hair, slicking it back on the sides until it gleamed. "I'm not being dragged anywhere. Whatever questions you answer with Dr. Curtis, you still need to answer with me. We need to talk too."

"About what?"

"Hell, I don't know." He got off the bed to pace. "Tell me about your previous relationships."

"What's to tell? Men either leave me, or I push them away."

"Why?"

"That's the big question."

"And your father?" He was no dummy. He hadn't missed her remark about his being dead. He just hadn't known how to bring it up before.

"He left me."

"You and your mother, you mean?"

"Right." Actually, it was wrong. He'd left *her*, in a bus depot in Pennsylvania somewhere. She was nine. It was the last time she'd seen him. That's what she remembered most.

Cally sat on the edge of the bed, her shriveled black nylons more than she could tackle right now. Steve stood by the door. If she ended up alone, it was because she was pushing him away. It took strength, and faith, but she reached out her hand. He sat beside her.

"Tell me what you need."

"Just don't leave me," she said.

"I won't."

Maybe he meant it. For now. But nothing was forever. Maybe, if she could be strong enough, she could love him for as long as he needed her. As long as it lasted. A cleft of pain in her heart whispered that for her, that might mean forever. "Hold me?"

He did.

She took a deep breath. In the name of honesty there were two things she had to say. "I love you. And it scares me."

"I won't leave." With a breath like a vow he promised. Then he sealed it with a touch and a kiss.

Come Sunday night, Steve had every intention of seeing her off in a cab. That's what he told himself as they pulled away from the curb, his arm around her in the backseat.

"Steve? Why is it I always share taxis with you?"

"I sent you off alone once, I don't plan on doing it again."

"Outside Lincoln Center." She remembered. "Was it that hard?"

"You know damn well it was." Tilting her face to his, he kissed her for all the time they'd lost between then and the previous night. He'd meant it to be one more good-night kiss as he saw her off. It turned into something more.

Eventually, Steve came up for air. "Speaking of romantic, I don't know how you feel about groping in the back of a cab." Never mind that his hands itched to do more.

"I never knew you were so shy," Cally said slyly, slipping her fingers into the opening between two of his shirt buttons. "After this morning, I thought you'd try anything."

"The driver—" The rest of his words were lost in a rush of breath as her tongue followed her fingers.

Steve dragged his attention back to the driver, whose dreadlocks bounced to the rhythm of a boom box on the front dash. The music could have been African jungle drums. It could have been Steve's pulse.

Distracting himself from the sensations Cally was wantonly calling forth, he tried to read the man's name on his license. It was almost nine o'clock, too dark. He and Cally had been together twenty-four wonderful, exhilarating, exhausting hours. And this incredible woman wasn't slowing down.

The cab bumped to a halt at a light.

"I should have called a limo," Steve said huskily, "we could've drawn the curtains."

With a brief, careless glance Cally noted the driver and the smudged and scratched Plexiglas divider. "Think he cares?"

"Probably not, if he's driven a cab in New York for more than a week."

She giggled, which sent a dozen more sensations revving through his nervous system.

He fumbled for the window crank, a blast of cold air mixing with the stuffiness the taxi heater blew out. "If you don't want me disgracing you in a public conveyance, you'd better stop."

"What happened to my adventurous Romeo? My savage? I never dreamed you had this streak of prudery."

That he'd never dreamed she could be this wild was supposed to have been his reply. Nothing came of it, not once he opened his eyes to watch her lips form around each syllable of the word *prudery*. The woman was a walking fantasy.

The radio blared.

"I love that music," she whispered in his ear.

"What music?"

"It makes me think of humidity, sweat. Primitive dancing rites, the young males of the tribe presenting themselves to their choice of mate."

"Fertility rites?"

They both imagined the darkness of a hut, fluttering torch flames, the conflagration of a bonfire.

"Fertility," she murmured vaguely, pausing.

He grunted. "I don't suppose even we could get that inventive in a taxi."

"I might think of something."

He groaned. "You know, for five minutes this morning I thought you were shy."

Suddenly they hit a puddle of water, and white spray exploded around them.

The driver was jabbering, gesturing out the window.

Cally chuckled. "Is he kicking us out of his cab?"

"The street's flooded," he replied. "Broken water main, I think."

"Not again," she said with a moan.

Outside there was at least half a foot of swirling water rushing around their tires. The cabdriver tried to back up, but the traffic behind him refused to cooperate.

"Brake, man," the driver said, turning toward them. "Brake, man."

"I don't know anything about brakes," Steve replied. "That's what Mercedes mechanics are for."

"Do you think he means there's something wrong with them?"

"Could be. Especially if they get this wet. I don't think he's going to take us anywhere right now."

The driver was hanging out his open window, deep in animated conversation with two other taxi drivers, none of them speaking in English.

Steve quickly surveyed the scene, spotting a blue neon sign. Tossing a five through the opening in the Plexiglas, he rolled up his pant cuffs and handed Cally his shoes and socks. "Here we go."

Stepping into the swirling cold, he picked her up and carried her through the water to the sidewalk.

Ten

"Now this is romantic." Cally laughed.

"Me standing here with my pants rolled up like Li'l Abner?" He set her down, hopping on one foot as he pulled on his socks and shoes. Then he nodded toward the neon sign.

It was a club, dark inside with a curved bar made of glass blocks. It was way too early for the disco-hopping regulars; they were almost the only customers.

"Why don't you set your coat here," he said, stopping by a table and stripping off a glove. "Damn." The other one was still in the taxi. "I'm going to look like Michael Jackson."

"Michael Jackson as a corporate raider, perhaps." Cally sidled up to him, running her hands up the lapels of the sport coat he'd thrown on. The man could wear anything from a suit to a ratty pair of sweats, and he still looked like something from GQ. "What next, Sir Walter?"

They had two choices, both painfully obvious. "We either sit, me with the tablecloth covering my lap, or we dance." Steve indicated the dance floor with a nod of his head.

Cally nodded slowly in return, unable to fathom how the man made his blue eyes smolder. She let him lead her onto the floor as a slow song played.

Front to front, heat to heat, they danced. She licked her lips, watching a tray of drinks go by.

"Stop that." Steve's voice ground.

"I wouldn't be *that* brazen."

"No? Lady, tonight anything you did wouldn't surprise me."

A flicker of humor lit her eyes.

Steve squeezed her hand and stopped moving. "Don't even think of it."

"Of what?" she asked innocently.

"Of whatever you can do to surprise me. We're here to work off the aftereffects of your last inventive idea."

She glanced away shyly.

"I now have material for a year of fantasies, thanks to you."

"Is that what you've been getting by on these last few years?"

"More or less." He stared into her eyes. So blue, so happy. He didn't want to think about the mistakes she'd made with men, so he didn't ask. How could he regret that experience when she'd found a happy ending with him?

When the dance had begun, their hands had been in the classic extended position. But he'd tugged her closer, their bodies moving gently, her hand tucked against his lapel. It wasn't long before the slow, languid motion had him hot and anxious and eager for her all over again. "I want you, Cally," he whispered. In a hundred ways, for a hundred years. In his life forever.

"Then what are we doing here?" she responded, aware of the desire growing between them, stunned that she could need him so much.

"We're waiting for me to cool down so I can walk

you to the curb without embarrassing both of us."

"And you're going to cool down this way?"

Steve became aware of how tightly he was pressed against her. "Let's grab a table."

They sat, Cally sweeping a lock of thoroughly ruffled hair off her cheek.

"Give me a minute, and I'll take you home," he said, signaling the waiter.

Cally ordered soda water. The next day was a workday. It was time she got home. The question of Steve's staying the night still lingered. "Steve?" She looked up.

"Don't bother asking. I need to get up in the morning too."

The way he read her mind unnerved her. "I wasn't inviting, I mean, I don't want you to think I'm making demands on you."

"Don't worry, you won't chase me away."

"You're entirely free to come and go." Just don't go yet, she prayed.

He reached across the table, clenching her hand in his. "I'm not going anywhere, baby."

Monday night Cally was beat. Steve hadn't called since dropping her off the previous night. She hadn't expected him to. He'd promised her some time for all this to sink in, breathing space, thinking that's what she needed. Steve, who believed in love. And Cally, who believed there were no easy answers, only difficult, irrevocable choices.

Grabbing a can of tomato juice from the fridge, Cally noticed the blinking light on her answering machine. Her heart leapt almost painfully, and a smile lit up her face. Part of her wished it wouldn't. Her happiness couldn't rely on phone calls from Steve. Perspective was what she needed.

The moment she heard her mother's voice, it was precisely what she got.

"I found your father."

Not again. Cally squeezed her eyes shut, opened them to punch out the number, then let it ring. Why did her mother persist in tracking down her father? How many months had gone by this time? How many years? She sighed heavily. That was her mother's problem, not hers.

She began speaking the moment her mother answered. "Mom, obviously you don't want him back."

"Of course not, honey. I just feel better knowing where he is."

Her mother thought of him as if he were one of her chicks, always looked after. "You're the original mother hen, you know that?" But they'd played this game before. Cally knew when to wait for the other shoe to drop.

"Your birthday is coming up," her mother said.

"Mom, I'm going to be thirty." It was more a warning than a statement.

"So it'd be a good time for him to call. I'm sure he'd like to know how you're doing."

And Cally was equally sure he wouldn't even remember if her mother didn't remind him. "How much have you paid private detectives over the years?"

"That's none of your business, sweetheart. But speaking of money, are you still seeing that doctor?"

Now it was her mother's turn to change the subject. Conversations with her mother were always haphazard, filled with emotional ups and downs, and logical ins and outs.

"A psychiatrist can't be cheap," her mother continued. "Do you need help?"

"Not the financial kind. Please, Mom, it's okay."

"I'm sorry, Cally."

Catching the tremble in her mother's voice, Cally felt a stab of guilt. "This is not an indictment of you as a mother. You don't have to apologize for anything."

"If I did something wrong—I tried to raise you the best I could . . ."

"It's not your fault you and Dad couldn't work things out. The past is over." Except when you tracked it down with private detectives, Cally didn't add. "I'm seeing Dr. Curtis to work some things out, that's all. Talk things over."

"But wouldn't it help to talk them over with your father? These things always have something to do with childhood, you know. I could call him for you."

"You don't have to fight my dragons for me, okay?" *Or get my father to call me or remind him I exist or patch up all the things that can't be patched up.* "I have to do these things for myself."

"Then, will you talk to him? Mark says he's—"

"Mark?"

"The detective I hired. He's a single man—he lives in a bungalow in Brooklyn, a pretty little house."

"Dad, you mean?"

"No, Mark. Your father's in another one of his boardinghouses. You'll meet him on Friday when you come to dinner. Mark, that is."

Now her mother was dating the man she'd

hired to find her ex-husband! What a family. At least Cally would have something interesting to tell Dr. Curtis.

There was a knock at the door. "Mom? I gotta go."

She peeped through the peephole and saw nothing but a bouquet of roses. Steve. Her heart fluttered and her veins heated and she knew she was entirely too happy to see him. "I thought we were going to play this casual for a couple days?" She was trying, though Lord knew her heart wasn't cooperating.

"Your doorman buzzed me through."

"I don't have a doorman."

"Okay, your downstairs neighbor. She thinks you should date more."

"Mrs. Kaminski! Why is it everyone wants to solve my problems lately? Not that I'm complaining right this minute." She twined her arms around his neck, their mouths meeting in a heat-seeking kiss.

"Now about this problem you have with shyness." He chuckled, lifting her in his arms to carry her across the room.

"Steve! You're going to rupture yourself."

"You're not exactly petite, are you?"

"Be very careful how you choose your words. I may not be small, but I'm sensitive."

"And I know where." He laid her on the bed, laughing and touching. "Here." Her breath caught. "And here." She mewed, a sleepy smile stealing across her face.

"Steve, what are you doing here?"

"Loving you."

That said it all.

* * *

"You're looking very happy today, Cally."

"Well, Dr. Curtis, a lot has happened since I last talked to you. I told you about Steve."

"Your wanted poster and occasional escort?"

"He's become a—a little more than that."

Dr. Curtis smiled. "A relationship?"

"We're lovers. At least, he says he loves me." And proved it every time he touched her.

"How do you feel about that?"

"Good." She said it definitely, with lots of emphasis. "Great." That sounded even more convincing. She loosened her grip on the tissue and attached a smile.

"That's good, Cally." The doctor could have sounded a little more enthusiastic.

"In fact, I'm thinking of canceling the rest of our meetings," Cally added, although the thought had just occurred to her.

"That happens," the doctor said, taking it in stride.

"People do get cured, you mean."

"Sometimes people stop coming because they think they're cured. How do you feel about not coming?"

"Relieved." It was the first word that popped into her head. It sounded rude, and it wasn't entirely the case.

"We've been getting into some painful issues. It's understandable that you want to avoid them. Or do you feel we've worked through them?"

Cally stepped carefully. "I feel different around Steve. More in control." Or so she had before she'd told him she loved him. That scared feeling didn't automatically go away.

"Do I detect doubts?"

"I've been doubting love since I was nine." She laughed. "It takes a while to get used to it."

"Your were nine when your father left."

"That's just a number I picked. It was a joke."

"The past has a way of intruding on the present."

Cally was on the edge of her seat. She consciously sat back, crossed her legs, and set her hands on the armrests. "Let's confront this directly, all right? Steve is different from my father. He's dedicated to his job and to me. My father was a drifter. He always had a new job, a new address."

And an excuse. Why he hadn't called. Why he wouldn't be stopping by. Why he hadn't bought her a present. Next year, baby, next year.

"I've fallen in love with Steve with my eyes open. I'm not a child anymore. If anyone left me in a bus station, I'd find my own way home."

They sat. A clock ticked. The doctor's voice was no louder. "Is that what happened?"

For some bizarre reason Cally suddenly felt like crying.

"Your mother will come get you," he'd said. She could still hear him, see the shadow of beard on his face, the smell of his shaving cream. He had dark heavy brows, dark eyes, and breath that smelled of cigars and coffee. "You stay here like a good girl. I gotta go."

She'd sat there for hours. Afraid to look up at the clock—big hands and little hands and hers tightly folded in her lap. To this day she disliked large round clocks with white faces.

She'd been so afraid. Afraid he'd left her for good. Afraid. And alone.

Haltingly, Cally told the story. "Mom's kept in touch with him all this time, getting him to call me. Can't we just lay it to rest? There's no way to make up for twenty years of neglect. I'd rather concentrate on Steve, on making that work."

"You can't guarantee he won't leave too."

Cally felt a finger of ice down her back and sat up straighter. "I know there aren't any guarantees. But Steve is different. He calls because he wants to. Spends time with me despite how busy he is at work. He doesn't make excuses. If we can be honest, this will work."

He called, he didn't come over. Feeling disappointed was unreasonable, and Cally was trying very hard to be reasonable. Love didn't have to mean hearts and flowers all the time.

"You didn't tell me your birthday was coming up," he said.

She cursed silently at how quickly he picked up on things. "I didn't want to fish for presents." The soft voices of Cary Grant and Deborah Kerr discussing a shipboard romance doomed to end wafted from the television in the background. "I don't want you to feel obligated."

A two-syllable curse of his own told her what he thought of that.

"Besides, I knew you'd want to buy me an outrageously expensive gift," she cooed into the receiver, turning a too sensitive area into an offhand joke.

She got away with it. Steve's no-nonsense reply told her so. "When exactly?"

"April Fools' Day. And no snickering." She wanted to tickle the hairs on the back of his neck, skim his chest with her nails, touch him, be with him. She also wanted to fight the urge to ask him to come over. He'd been busy at work the entire week.

"I'll send you something," he said. "Promise."

It was not a word Cally liked. Too often it had been matched with the word *broken*.

"Can't you drop it off?" she asked. Now she was fishing for visits.

His pause took a fraction too long. Cally felt her stomach tighten and didn't know why. Then he spoke. "I'll be out of town. Spur of the moment thing, don't know when I'll be back."

She fought the all-too-familiar feelings. It was only a business trip. It wasn't as if he were disappearing from her life. So why did she get the sense there was more he wasn't saying? "You could have said it without my having to drag it out of you."

She was mad at him. Steve sighed silently. Why was it, no matter how much you loved a woman, she got mad if you left? "Look, you know about the promotion. Flying off to Europe at the last minute is as much a test of my dedication as those visits to a shrink."

Dammit, he thought. He was letting the irritation show. If he didn't like the way he sounded, he was sure she wouldn't. He also didn't like having to justify the fact that he was committed to his job.

"I'm sorry, babe. I should have told you sooner, but I didn't know when we'd get the go-ahead. We have this agreement to hammer out with the Dutch over currency exchange as part of a takeover package. It shouldn't be more than a few weeks. We'll celebrate when I get back."

She shut her eyes tight, her hand clutching the receiver. All the big plans, big deals that couldn't wait.

"I love you. I'll be back." He just didn't love having to prove it and not knowing why. "Cally." He sighed into the phone. "Talk to me. Please."

Excuses. Endearments. Promises. Now Cally remembered why she didn't like promises.

"I'll bring you something."

"I'm not a child, Steve."

"I didn't mean it that way. I want to, dammit." Steve rubbed his forehead. Her coolness made it even tougher. If only he could be there, find out what was wrong. "You know I'd rather be with you. What's the matter?"

She would not cling. She would not cry. Not on the phone. There was a simple explanation. He had business to conduct. It wasn't his fault she'd heard this one too many times. "I'm overreacting. I'm going to miss you, that's all."

"I don't know if I'll be able to call much. The time difference is a bear, and Marty is into power breakfasts. I'll probably come home fat."

Come home? She tried not to laugh, but the bitter smile wouldn't leave her mouth, the voice of a too knowing child reverberating in her head. She'd believe it when she saw it.

"We'll talk as soon as I get back. I have to go. I love you."

Part of her knew that was true. Part of her was dying. "Good-bye, Steve."

Ridiculous, she thought, to hold on to the receiver so long after the line went dead. But as long as she didn't hang up, the phone call wasn't over, nothing was officially over.

She didn't know whom she was talking to as

she watered her plants, she just had to put it in words. "He's different, remember? Just because he goes rushing off on a business scheme—"

Scheme? That's a multibillion-dollar international conglomerate.

"Besides, he loves me."

He's leaving.

"He'll be back."

Isn't that what they all say?"

"Look, if you can't deal with a simple business trip, maybe you're not ready for a relationship of any kind."

A few weeks at most, the hopeful part of her said. He was different, and she loved him.

Nevertheless, the small voice from long ago kept repeating, "But he'll miss my birthday."

The last-minute hysteria that accompanied every edition of the *Journal for Policy Issues in Political Science* had passed. April's edition was in the mail. Things would be quiet for several more weeks while people prepared their stories for the next edition. Worn out, Cally trudged home through streets washed with warm April rain.

That night she awoke to the sound of the phone's ringing in the living room. Her digital alarm clock read 4:42 A.M. She let her machine pick it up. A voice spoke softly for a few minutes. She got out of bed.

"What time is it there, Cal? Have you changed to daylight saving time yet? I can never remember."

Steve. Her heart felt as if it were being squeezed by a fist. She missed him so much. He sounded tired. The light was just beginning to creep through the window.

"It's late morning. I thought that'd make it almost five there. Don't want to wake you, and there's no sense in your calling back since we're leaving today for Belgium. Thought I'd just leave a message. I love you. And no, I didn't forget your birthday. I've got your present here. I thought it best not to mail it. If you want to write me, though, send it to the office or the Sheraton, Brussels. Love you."

He hung up.

Cally knew she couldn't get back to sleep now. Her finger stopped on the rewind button.

Wandering around the apartment, flicking on a light in the kitchen, she listened to the buzz of the fluorescent tube, the whoosh of the water faucet spurting its first water of the day. She made coffee. Water sifted through the filter and the grounds as if the machine were sorting something out. Slowing dripping coffee hit the pot with thudding drops, then became a steady stream, as if the machine had decided something.

This was the second time Steve had called. He was busy. He apologized for missing her calls. She wondered if he was as aware as she that she hadn't made any, hadn't even tried leaving a message at his office. There were so many things she wanted to tell him that just wouldn't work on an answering machine. She wanted to prove she could live without him. She wouldn't cling. He didn't have to know she listened to his messages over and over, that her faith in him was often as shaky as her doubts.

He didn't have to know the doubts were winning. But she'd have to tell him. Soon.

She sat at the table crammed into the end of the kitchen alcove and looked at the bricks across the air shaft. She had a typewriter set up there with some paper and a half dozen reference books. None of them told her what she needed to know.

She rolled a piece of paper through the platen. She'd always thought better on paper. Staring at the blank white, stomach churning for that first hit of caffeine, she began to type.

It all came down to one thing. She didn't trust him. No, that wasn't it. She didn't trust. That was it. Didn't trust that love would last. Steve might mean everything he said. He might even be the type to keep promises, to not pull away when love got too close, when the word *commitment* was spoken. But *she* didn't believe. Someday, it would fall apart. Someday, he would go and not come back.

So she typed the letter.

> I'm sorry, Steve. This won't work. I'm too mixed up right now. The past, the present. Dr. Curtis was right all along. I should have given up on men entirely until I solved my problems, or at least knew how to live with them. I knew she was right, but I didn't want to see it. You were right about our having this time apart.
>
> I'm glad we had what we had. But I need to solve my own problems. I loved you too. Please don't call or try to change my mind, this is hard enough. If I ever get the courage, I'll call you.

Three nights after she mailed the letter, in care of his New York office, the phone rang.

"Steve."

"What's that banging noise?"

Only my heart. "The plumbing."

"Great place you got there."

Empty place. "Where are you?"

"Paris. Stopover. Waiting for Eurorail."

"Ah." Had he got her letter? Why didn't he mention it? She waited, her heart clattering in her chest like the heating registers.

"I miss you."

The words were difficult to hear over the roar of a train coming into the station. They were impossible to ignore.

"I miss you too," she said, squeezing her eyes tightly shut. "I, I'm sorry we fought, about your going so suddenly."

"That was a fight?" He laughed. "I've been categorizing it as a tiff." Categorizing, cauterizing, mulling, and worrying like a ninny in love. In short, he hadn't stopped thinking about her for so much as an hour.

"You get my phone messages?"

"Yes. You didn't get my letter yet?"

She'd written him? His heart soared. He'd been worried, needlessly it appeared, over the fact she hadn't called. The things love would do to an otherwise sane man. "Did you send it here or to my office? It'd get here quicker if you went through the office."

"You told me that. That's what I did."

"Hope you didn't cover it with kisses, I'd never live it down with the secretarial pool."

"No, I didn't."

"Perfume?"

"Sorry." This time the smile was bittersweet. She'd ended their relationship, convinced she

had to solve her problems alone, and he didn't
know it yet. Was it wrong to hold on to one more
conversation, one more chance to hear his voice,
imagine his smile?

"You know," he said as quietly as he could manage in the hustle of the station, "you could've
faxed it."

Her heart shriveled. "No, I don't think so."

"It was that good, huh?"

It felt good to hear his voice, even better to hear
his laughter. If only he hadn't left, if they'd had
more time, they could have worked things out,
gotten on firmer ground. This should have been
good-bye, why did he have to sound so happy simply to be talking to her?

"Not a bad connection for transatlantic," she
croaked out, her throat tightening with every
word.

"You answered so fast. Were you sleeping on
the couch?"

"I drifted off." For the third time this week. It
was easier than facing a bed that had learned his
imprint, his smell on the pillowcase.

A train whistle pierced the air like a cry.

"Gotta go," he said. "Cally, I'm sorry we got off
to a bad start this trip. I'll be back when I can.
I'll write."

"Sure. Go."

"I love you."

She bit her lip. For one last time, for all the
times, she said, "I love you too."

"Mind my calling you at work?"

"No." She got up to close the door to her office.

"I missed you, and this looked like the only time I'd get off today."

Cally closed her eyes and sat back in her creaky chair. One more day, one more call. How long did overseas mail take? But for now she had a reprieve. On this one day, when she knew she desperately needed to talk to someone, Steve was there.

"How's it going?"

"I went to see my father," she said.

There was a short pause on his end. "Yeah?"

"For breakfast. It was the only time he had free."

"That couldn't have been easy. Want to talk about it?"

"At a dollar a minute?" She tried to laugh. She wanted not to cry.

"Talk to me, Cally."

Eleven

Leaning on his steady support, she told him, sorting it out while the tangled emotions were still fresh.

"I wasn't sure what to call him. 'Dad' sounded too familiar." Instead she'd said simply, "Glad you could make it."

They'd met in a doughnut place in Queens. Her father looked as if he spent a lot of mornings there, smoking and drinking coffee, chatting with the policemen getting ready for their morning rounds. The waitresses all knew his name.

"Meet my daughter, Rose. Grown up some, hasn't she?"

The waitress nodded without looking up. "You want decaf, honey?"

"Regular will be fine."

Cally had talked this over with her mother, with Dr. Curtis, with everyone but Steve. Now he was the first to hear the results. How her father had said, "Your Mom mentioned your birthday was coming up. Gotcha a little something. I know it's late."

About twenty-one years too late, Cally had thought, then regretted it. She wasn't there to accuse, but to understand.

He'd reached into his tatty sport coat with its

wide lapels. His heavy dark brows were shot with gray. His face had filled out some, although she couldn't say for sure. A copy of the racing form sat neatly folded on the side of the table. She saw three horses' names marked off in pencil.

He slid a slim box across the table. For a moment Cally thought it was cigars. "For me?"

"Yeah. Open it."

Her hands didn't shake, not until the box was open. It was a charm bracelet, pewter, laid on a folded piece of gauze. She could have been nine years old all over again. On the phone with Steve, Cally glanced at her purse. She hadn't taken the box out since leaving the restaurant.

"Didn't know if you still liked those or not," her father had said, poking a finger at the bracelet. "That one says '30' on it."

Cally had swallowed the lump in her throat, setting the box down and folding her shaking hands in her lap. "Daddy, Dad, I wanted to talk about some things. I want you to know I'm not going to track you down like Mom has."

"Your mom, well, that's how that is, isn't it?"

"Yes, well, I'm not interested." She paused.

"Is that all you told him?" Steve asked.

Cally rubbed the knot of tension at the back of her neck. "I asked him why he left. That's what I was there for."

"What did he say?"

In her memory she could still see him stirring his coffee with a wooden stirrer, then chewing it for a few minutes like a large toothpick. "Water under the bridge, baby," he'd said.

Five thousand miles away, Steve cursed softly. "That was it?"

"He said sometimes it was easier to leave than

go on hurting people." Cally thought of the letter she'd written Steve. Hadn't her excuse been the same? She was leaving him because she had things to work out on her own, yet here she was telling him the whole story, hanging on his every word, *needing* him.

"He said I was too little to understand at the time. It wasn't my fault."

"Of course it wasn't."

"But children can put a strain on any marriage, especially when there are money problems too."

"And whose fault was that? His? The horses?"

"Steve."

"What?"

Tell him, a voice cried out. *Tell him what's coming.* She'd made the worst mistake of her life, pushing him away before he could leave her. But the words wouldn't come out. "Thanks for being there," she said instead, hoping he didn't hear the choking in her voice.

"That's why I'm here, babe."

"I wasn't there to blame him, I just had to know." And to ask about the bus station.

"The bus station?" The older man had grinned when he'd said it, as if it were some old family story he'd lost track of. Then a light bulb came on. "The *bust* station. Remember when I used to call it that? Every time I was flat on my back out of cash, I'd end up there. Had you with me one time, did I?"

"You left me there by myself. I was nine."

A plate of eggs and sausage had arrived. He sprinkled them with pepper. "Long time ago, twinkle toes. Long time ago."

"I was scared."

"You were a little kid." He shrugged. As if that

explained everything. "Can't be hauling you around some of the places I used to go. You was better off with your mother, I always knew that. She came and picked you up, didn't she?"

"Yes."

"So what was the story?"

The story, quite simply, was that she'd lived her life around it. Burying it, denying it, hating, forgiving, wondering why, and blaming herself.

A train whistled, drawing her back to the present. "Steve?"

"I'm still here."

"Do you have to go?"

"Not yet."

"We didn't talk much after that." It had become painfully obvious that she and her father were strangers in a restaurant, trying to make conversation. More than once Cally had had to follow his glance to the racing form and back. "If you want to get going . . ." She had pulled out her wallet.

"Here now, the least I can do for my little girl." He'd looked at the grown woman his daughter had become, his shoulders hunched as he'd patted his pockets for change. Then he'd set down fifty extra cents for her coffee. "Take care of yourself."

Hadn't she always? Until someone like Steve Rousseau came along and tried to be there for her, and she'd sent him away.

"Honey, I have to go," Steve said. "It couldn't have been easy, seeing him after all this time. I'm proud of you, I want you to know that."

So was she, to a point. There'd been no emotional outbursts, no startling discoveries beyond the fact that her parents had split up long ago, and she'd grown up with her mother. Was that so unusual? And Steve loved her. Why was that so hard to believe? She'd faced the past but had feared the future. So she'd canceled it, with a letter, and no matter how she wanted to, there was no way to undo it.

"Have a nice trip," she said, trying to get off the phone before the tears started.

"Is that it?"

She had a terrible sinking feeling it could be. "I—I have to go." Her hand rested on the receiver long after she'd set it back in the cradle. "Oh, Cally, how could you?"

The tulips were waiting on the landing. They meant Steve was in Holland, although the delivery tag said "FTD, NYC."

A passel of postcards fell out of her mailbox, scrawled in airports, dashed off on his knee under the table at business meetings, all mailed to his office to be forwarded locally. They were like his phone calls, sweet, funny, to the point. He never failed to say he loved her.

Busy. Have nagging feeling you were mad at me for leaving. Tell me, Doc, when I got off the plane, my feet didn't quite touch the ground. Could it be love? Is there a cure? Looking forward to bed rest and TLC when I return. Love you, Steve.

Writing this in back of cab on way to Hilton. That black line was a swerve for a bike. Low clouds, rain. What else is new in Amsterdam? Missing you, that's what. Home ASAP. Love, Steve.

Conference room, government building, The Hague. Plane going overhead just now. Pictured me on it, coming back to you. Better yet, us returning for honeymoon. Your input please on the above (business joke). Love you very much (no joke). Steve.

Wish these things weren't so public. I'd tell you what I was really thinking during a seminar on Common Market Ramifications to Currency Regulation. Will have to demonstrate when I get home. Hot for you, Steve.

For a researcher, you're not much of a letter writer. How about postcards? NY is full of them: Trump Tower, Times Square, Statue of Liberty. Send some. Send love. I'm sending flowers. And don't tell me the U.S. Post Office is snowed under with tax returns. Love, Steve.

How long does overseas mail take, anyway? Too little space to waste complaining at lack of response. Write me care of office, and it'll be forwarded in company packet. Thought I explained before I left. Will probably get whole packet from you at next destination. Looks like a couple more weeks here. This card from Netherlands museum. Dutch masters not known for their erotic art. (Unlike my dreams of you.) Love, Steve.

That phone call about your Dad was probably the most reasonable item on my expense account, so don't worry. Easily the most important. Glad I could be there for you.

Proud of you. Wish I could hold you. Always loving you. Steve.

Then nothing. He'd gotten the letter.

"Dr. Curtis!"

Martha Curtis hadn't heard her name spoken like an accusation in at least a week. She reached for the notepad beside her phone. "May I ask who's speaking?"

"Rousseau, Steven. Former patient of yours."

"You sound unhappy, Mr. Rousseau."

"If unhappy is a euphemism for mighty damned teed off, you got it right the first time."

"And might I ask why?"

"Your patient, Cally Baldwin."

Dr. Curtis paused. "I don't discuss patients, Mr. Rousseau. Not that I'm saying I even know this person."

"You know her. You're the one who told her to stop seeing me. Again. She's called it off, dammit." Steve knew he sounded ridiculous blaming this woman for his own failures. He should have been there, not running around Europe racking up points with the big boys. But dammit, what had he done wrong? There was only one person who could tell him.

"You're a friend of Miss Baldwin's?" Dr. Curtis asked.

"I'm the man who loves her."

The doctor's eyes grew wide. So this was the Steve whom Cally Baldwin had been crying about the last two weeks. The doctor ran through a few possibilities in her mind, then stretched toward the credenza and retrieved his folder. "I can dis-

cuss *you*, Mr. Rousseau, not any other patients."
She flipped through his folder. "Is this the one
who wanted to be just friends? The challenge?"

"Yes." He added a few expletives for emphasis.

"I see you won her over." From her tone, that
didn't sound entirely complimentary.

"I continued to date her, if that's what you
mean. Despite your contract." He couldn't have
made the last word more sarcastic. "Except for
phone calls *I* initiated, I haven't heard from her
since I left for Europe. Then the only mail I get is
a Dear John letter. What does this mean?"

"Mr. Rousseau, there's not much I—"

"Why is she doing this? I *know* she's discussed
it with you." It hurt too much to say the rest of
it. That she should have discussed it with him
instead of turning to a third party. But that was
the way it was; he'd have to deal with it.

"Why don't you ask her?" Dr. Curtis asked
gently.

"I plan to. But first I want to run it by you and
find out what's going on." He cursed again, but
this time it was directed at himself. "I don't want
to hurt her."

Martha Curtis subtly relaxed into the long
pause on the other end of the line. She'd been
waiting for something besides territorial line-
drawing. After fifteen years in this profession she
recognized sincerity.

"I know she has problems," Steve said. "She
told me about meeting her father again. I thought
we were getting somewhere. Is this how you solve
her problems, getting her to stop seeing me?"

"Cally makes her own decisions, Mr.
Rousseau."

"But you agreed."

He was as quick to pounce on an opening as a cross-examining attorney. Dr. Curtis picked her words carefully. "As I recall from my notes, you suspected your love was all she needed to get over her problems."

All right, so he'd been a fool, patting himself on the back for being everything the woman needed. He'd been berating himself ever since he'd gotten Cally's letter. He didn't need Martha Curtis's rubbing it in.

He'd been pompous and self-important, convinced he alone could cure her, a Prince Charming who had woefully misread the signals. He'd failed her, and she was cutting him loose. That couldn't be the end of it.

The silence continued. Dr. Curtis heard office activity in the background, the purr of an intercom, the summons of a page. Finally, Steve spoke.

"From what I can gather, she's decided to take up this cockamamy contract business again and swear off men."

"And what are you going to do about that, Steve?"

"Barge in and demand an explanation." He was dangerously close to doing just that, scene or no scene.

"Does she want to see you?"

"Not according to her letter, but that was written three weeks ago."

"Do you think she's changed her mind?"

"How would I know? I can't get in touch with her. You'd know."

"But I can't tell you."

Steve stopped pacing off the length of his desk long enough to sink into the large leather chair.

One fist clenched and unclenched on his knee. His nerves felt as if his secretary had fed them through the office shredder. His head pounded, his back was knotted up, and for some damned reason, there was an ache precisely where his heart was. "You know how she feels. And I don't."

Dr. Curtis sounded sincere in her apology. "My hands are tied, Steve. I can't tell you what we say here."

He knew that. But that was the first and last place Cally would go to talk things over.

Hanging up with a blunt good-bye, Steve stuffed his briefcase with papers. He gave his secretary a phone number and told her to keep calling it; he'd be gone for the afternoon. He was exhausted from the time change, his body was coiled with anger and frustration, and his emotions were edging on despair. He had to talk to Cally. He couldn't lose her. But first, he was going to work out until every muscle howled or gave up.

Putting all thoughts on hold, Steve sliced through the indoor pool at the club, the backwash rippling off the tiles, his arms pumping. Getting Cally Baldwin back was his only goal. Emotions mattered most, but he would need a strategy. If he was going to make the right decisions, he'd have to be cool, sharp, rested. Unlike any business deal he'd ever negotiated, this time his heart, his life, were on the line.

Cordelia dumped a pile of *Herald Tribune*s on the floor and sat her plump posterior on the corner of Cally's desk. "Gloomy in here."

Cally glanced around the dusky office and the

musty volumes on her shelves. "What else is new?"

"Smells too."

Cally glanced guiltily toward her wastebasket, saw no old lunches rotting, and sniffed. "Old print smells that way." Not that she would know, her nose had been stuffed up for a month. Crying did that.

"Have you got a secret admirer?" Cordelia asked blandly.

"Hardly." Maybe if she buried her nose in this newspaper, she could hide the hurt. She had no one. Her own insecurity had seen to that.

Cordelia studied her nails. "Is someone looking for you?"

Cally tried to fold the newspaper with as little rustling as possible. A shiver of fear suddenly held her nerves hostage. "Such as?"

"Didn't you get the message? A woman's been calling, asking if you're in."

Cally's heart left its place in her throat and dropped back to somewhere near her knees. "A woman."

"Whenever I tell her you're here, she hangs up."

At least this time Cally knew it wasn't a wife, as had been the case with Marlin. All those mistakes seemed so long ago. And so minor compared to the one she'd made with Steve. Cally picked up her purse. "Well, the next time she calls, tell her I'm out."

"Going somewhere?"

"Doctor appointment."

"These spring colds hang on forever."

Cally didn't bother correcting her misconception. "See you later."

*   *   *

Cally sat in Dr. Curtis's office, crying.

"Perhaps there's a deeper reason why you ended the relationship, something you sensed?"

"I was afraid he was leaving me. Isn't that what all men do, have done? So I pushed him away first. I told him I wasn't ready for a relationship. Don't call me, I'll call you. How's that for tact?"

The laughter was hollow coming from a tear-streaked face. "Maybe I wasn't ready. Maybe if I'd listened to you from the first and hadn't gotten involved, neither one of us would have been hurt.

"I still remember the sound of his voice on the answering machine the last time he called me. He sounded so hurt."

Got your letter, he'd said. *Don't worry, I won't bother you again.* She could understand the anger. It was the hurt and confusion beneath the surface that haunted her, and the fact that she loved him enough to recognize that. Oh, Lord, what had she done?

"He wasn't backing out! Before he got the letter, he called every other night, sent postcards, flowers. And all the time I knew it was over, but I couldn't tell him. Oh, Martha, what'll I do?" She blew her nose, hard.

Cally finished dabbing her eyes, ripping another tissue from the designer box.

The doctor waited. "Cally, would you mind going over your reasoning for writing the letter one more time?"

"I said I was swearing off men again, that I should have done that from the beginning. What I should have done was have my head examined!" She laughed halfheartedly and sniffed again.

"Did you think that was the best course under the circumstances?"

"Don't you?"

"I'm not sure I would have suggested a complete cessation this far along in the relationship. Perhaps talking it out would have been a better course."

"In other words, I blew it. I know that! Steve kept in touch with me more in the last six weeks than my father did in twenty years. But I couldn't believe that it wouldn't happen again. I didn't trust him or myself. It's all my fault."

Dr. Curtis kept her gaze on Cally. "Relationships are a two-way street. Don't you think some of this might be laid at Steve's door? Maybe he rushed you into a relationship you weren't ready for?"

Nineteen stories below, traffic was reduced to a distant hum as Cally gazed out the window from her seat. "I was ready for us to be lovers. I wanted it. It was the future I was afraid of. You know, a few weeks apart should have been a very good idea. It gave us time to adjust to the new level in our relationship."

"And?"

The sky was so blue, Cally thought. Was it that blue in Brussels? Was Steve still in Europe? He could be in New York, and she'd have no way of knowing. She closed her eyes to the pain. "He had no way of knowing that leaving was exactly the wrong thing to do. My fault again."

"Cally, do you love Steve?"

"Yes." The word was a drawn-out whisper.

"Then why haven't you called him?"

It was as difficult for Cally to say as it had been to admit all those lonely nights. "Maybe I don't deserve him. I pushed him away the first time I felt threatened. Maybe it *would* be better if we ended it. For his sake."

"But?"

Dr. Curtis jumped. Behind Cally's shoulder the door swung silently open. Steve Rousseau slipped in, shutting it without a sound. His hair was wet, slicked back but tousled, as if he'd run a hand through it impatiently, repeatedly.

Cally closed her eyes and straightened her shoulders. It hurt. The silence since he'd gotten her letter hurt. Every night when she came home, the emptiness of her apartment hurt. "But I still want to talk to him."

"Then talk," Steve ordered bluntly.

Twelve

Cally whirled around. "Steve!"

He didn't touch her. Instead he dragged up the matching wingback chair. He'd rarely asked for anyone's advice on his personal life, but this would be the second time in two days he'd asked for Dr. Curtis's opinion. "I think it's time we had some joint counseling, don't you?"

"When did you get back? How did you know I'd be here?" Cally's frantic glance at Dr. Curtis elicited a small shake of the head.

"I don't give out that information, Cally."

"I had my secretary call," Steve said. "She asked for you until someone told her you were out of the office for an hour. Then I put two and two together." Two and two. The world was made up of pairs. Couldn't she see they had to be together?

"Steve came to see me yesterday," Dr. Curtis added. "As for his walking in on a session, I can't condone that."

"But having one patient fall in love with another isn't exactly normal operating procedure, is it, Doc?" Steve plucked at a trouser seam before crossing his legs. He'd stared down tougher opponents, although the stakes had never been this high. "I want to marry Cally."

The doctor pursed her lips and looked at Cally. "Cally, you make your own decisions."

"I love her," Steve insisted. He sounded desperate, and his stomach was in knots. Worse, he was afraid to look at Cally just yet to see what her reaction would be. The whole thing was as bad as asking a father's permission.

"Love helps," the doctor replied noncommittally.

"I don't want to hurt her, but I insist on having a chance." He had to plead his case, to plead period. He was in over his head, but only one of the women in the room could pull him out. Finally, he looked at Cally. "I thought any hurts you had were *our* problems. We'd solve them together. Was that wishful thinking, Cally? Was I too damn cocky?"

His searing eyes never wavered, searching, asking, imploring, accusing. Cally's nerves were jangling like a horse-drawn sleigh. There were too many words she wanted to say just now, but none of them seemed to be making their way to her suddenly dry mouth.

"What was the letter for?" he asked, his voice grating on unspoken emotion.

"I thought it best," she said softly.

"And?"

"And I messed it up by still loving you." It didn't answer the question, but they were the only words that seemed to matter.

Steve got up, paced around her chair, the office, stopping for a long time by the rain-streaked window and looking down. She'd never know how much self-control it took for him not to cross-examine her. He wanted to take matters into his own hands. Shout orders. Decide, dammit! But he couldn't make her want him. Not forever. It was her choice, she had to make it alone. "If what you really want is not to hurt me, then don't send me away."

"I went to see my father," she began.

"You told me," he said softly.

"I had to know why he left me. Why everyone leaves me."

Steve bit back a curse, eager to strangle anyone who'd give a child that idea, much less a woman. "You told me it wasn't your fault, you learned that."

"I know." She smiled, and his heart turned over.

The view out the window was easier; he wouldn't let himself take it. He forced himself to continue facing her. "For that reason you wrote me off?"

"No!" She reached out.

He sunk his hands in his pockets. It was the only way to prevent himself from grabbing her hand, tugging her out of that chair, and holding on for dear life. He couldn't touch her yet.

So Cally slowly put her hand back in her lap, softly tearing the tissue. "By the time I realized it wasn't my fault, I'd already mailed the letter. I couldn't unwrite it. I sabotaged my own happiness, Steve. There has to be something wrong with a person who does that. Maybe it's better for you to know that."

For the first time Steve heard a clock ticking in the office. Or maybe it was his pulse kicking into overdrive.

Cally's eyes were drier now, steady on his. She saw the lines, the tension, the weariness. "I was protecting myself, cutting what I was sure were my losses. I didn't know when you left that you'd keep coming back."

"I'm persistent," he said, "it's one of my lovable qualities." It was also the quality that had kept him in Europe an extra week after her letter arrived, putting in eighteen-hour days, getting a deal locked up that would ensure his future at AmeriConGroup for years to come. But his real future was with her. How could he lock this one up? He fumbled with the box in his pocket.

"You look tired," she said softly.

"Time change," he grumbled.

She hiccuped and laughed. "Jet lag meets crying jag. What a pair we must make!"

"Quite a couple," he said, looking at her long and hard. He took a step, then another, still afraid to close the distance completely. "Tell me you love me again."

"I love you. And I'm so sorry."

That was all he needed to hear. He hauled her out of the chair, for the moment ignoring her startled cry of surprise, kissing her until her hair was mangled, her shoulders probably bruised by his grip. When he'd tasted all he could taste, filled his heart with everything he loved about her, he made her sit. How or when he got down on one knee, he never remembered. He just knew it was the best position from which to look her in the eye as he took the ring out of his pocket.

"A present from Amsterdam," he said, "diamond capital of the world."

She opened the small box and breathed his name. "Oh, Steve."

"Birthday present, engagement present, wedding present."

She blinked back the tears. He didn't give up,

did he? "You forgot April Fools' Day. Which is what I've been."

"Me too. As I said, we make quite a couple. But if you think you can leave me and I won't come after you, you've got a lot to learn about me."

"Like your stubborn streak?"

"Like my persistence."

"Bullheadedness."

"Call it devotion, and we've got a deal."

She smiled and nodded through new tears. "Deal."

He folded her hand around the box. "There're some other clauses we have to nail down here before we're done. Fidelity is one, but that shouldn't be a problem. It's the long-term partnership I'll need your okay on. I'm talking marriage, Cally."

"You picked a nice pose from which to ask me," Cally teased. "Do you always conduct business down on one knee?" For all her dreams, she'd never pictured Steve Rousseau that way.

"No, but it's how I clinch the deal. Say yes."

"Yes?"

He shook his head. It was the answer he wanted, but it lacked conviction. "No more doubts, Cally. I mean this." He had to grip her shoulders to prove it. His hands were shaking too much to take the ring out and put in on her finger. "Do you love me?"

"I don't want to hurt you."

"Then include me in your problems. Tell me what's wrong."

"Nothing, nothing at all." And that would be true as long as he was there. Cally curled her arms around his neck, hugging him until the chair arm pressed into her ribs. She was crying again. And hiccuping. And probably looked like hell.

"I should have taken you with me on that trip to Brussels," he said.

"I have a job."

"Will they give you time off for a honeymoon?"

"They'd better."

"How about a cruise? No interruptions, no business."

"Your company—"

"I'll disarm the ship-to-shore radio. They won't be able to reach me."

"What if the boat starts to sink?"

"Then you grab your three favorite movies and meet me on the nearest desert island."

"You'll bring the VCR?"

"Mmm-hmm. I'll join you under the waterfall, where the water will cascade down your body, washing away the sand." His hand made the motion. She felt a thundering rush in her veins.

"All that water will ruin the VCR," she whispered.

He kissed her on the mouth, the cheek, the top of her head. "No logic this time, this is our fantasy island. Anyway, we'll have better things to do than watch movies. As for your status as goddess, I'm going to be the one worshiping and cherishing. All those natives in their canoes will have to look elsewhere."

If Dr. Curtis was lost in their allusions, the kiss gave her time to glance at her watch. After three full minutes she cleared her throat. It only broke them apart far enough to stare into each other's eyes. They shared smiles; remembered pain, forgiveness, and desire passed between them.

And tenderness. Cally straightened Steve's tie.

It was so unlike him to be mussed. With his hands in her hair, holding her face up to his like a lost treasure, she knew mussed very well. Her face was tear streaked, eyes puffy, and lipstick gone. None of it mattered when he looked at her that way. "When do we start propagating the species on this desert island of ours?"

"The sooner the better," he replied.

"Uh, excuse me," Dr. Curtis asked, insinuating herself into the conversation, "but does this island you plan to live on have a name?"

"Manhattan," Steve replied as if it were perfectly obvious.

"Ah." Dr. Curtis nodded. It made sense. Right now they *were* the only two people on an island of millions, the only two people in the world.

"Promise me," Steve whispered harshly, staring into Cally's blue eyes, "promise me we can work anything out together. Just don't ever leave me out in the cold like that again."

Despite his hold, Cally shook her head vigorously. The word "never" was whispered passionately in reply, followed by a kiss and the words "yes" and "forever."

Not that Dr. Curtis could have sworn to the last part. Their mouths were obscured by kisses, lips pressed to lips. Waiting for a reasonable opportunity to interrupt, she contented herself with quietly closing the folder. Then, organized as ever, she scrawled a note to her secretary: *Keep my Saturdays free for June. I have a wedding to go to.*

THE EDITOR'S CORNER

Next month you have even more wonderful reading to look forward to from LOVESWEPT. We're publishing another four of our most-asked-for books as Silver Signature Editions, which as you know are some of the best romances from our early days! In this group you'll find **ONCE IN A BLUE MOON** (#26) by Billie Green, **SEND NO FLOWERS** (#51) by Sandra Brown, and two interrelated books—**CAPTURE THE RAINBOW** and **TOUCH THE HORIZON** by Iris Johansen. Those of you who haven't had the pleasure of savoring these scrumptious stories are in for one bountiful feast! But do leave room on your reading menu for our six new LOVESWEPTs, because they, too, are gourmet delights!

A new Iris Johansen book is always something to celebrate, and Iris provides you with a real gem next month. **TENDER SAVAGE,** LOVESWEPT #420, is the love story of charismatic revolutionary leader Ricardo Lazaro and daring Lara Clavel. Determined to free the man who saved her brother's life, Lara risks her own life in a desperate plan that takes a passionate turn. Trapped with Ricardo in his cramped jail cell, Lara intends to playact a seduction to fool their jailer—but instead she discovers a savage need to be possessed, body and soul, by her freedom fighter. Lara knew she was putting herself in jeopardy, but she didn't expect the worst danger to be her overwhelming feelings for the rebel leader of the Caribbean island. Iris is a master at developing tension between strong characters, and placing them in a cell together is one sure way to ignite those incendiary sparks. Enjoy **TENDER SAVAGE,** it's vintage Johansen.

Every so often a new writer comes along whose work seems custom-made for LOVESWEPT. We feel Patricia Burroughs is such a writer. Patricia's first LOVESWEPT is **SOME ENCHANTED SEASON,** #421, and in it she offers readers the very best of what you've come to expect in our romances—humor, tender emotion, sparkling dialogue, smoldering sensuality, carefully crafted prose, and characters who tug at your heart. When artist Kevyn Llewellyn spots the man who is the epitome of the warrior-god she has to paint, she can't believe her good fortune. But convincing him to pose for her is another story. Rusty Rivers thinks the lady with the silver-streaked hair is a kook, but he's irresistibly drawn to her nonetheless. An incredible tease, Rusty tells her she can use his body only if he can use hers! Kevyn can't

(continued)

deal with his steamy embraces and fiery kisses, she's always felt so isolated and alone. The last thing she wants in her life is a hunk with a wicked grin. But, of course, Rusty is too much a hero to take no for an answer! This story is appealing on so many levels, you'll be captivated from page one.

If Janet Evanovich weren't such a dedicated writer, I think she could have had a meteoric career as a comedienne. Her books make me laugh until I cry, and **WIFE FOR HIRE, LOVESWEPT #422**, is no exception. Hero Hank Mallone spotted trouble when Maggie Toone sat down and said she'd marry him. But Hank isn't one to run from a challenge, and having Maggie pretend to be his wife in order to improve his reputation seemed like the challenge of a lifetime. His only problem comes when he starts to falling in love with the tempting firecracker of a woman. Maggie never expected her employer to be drop-dead handsome or to be the image of every fantasy she'd ever had. Cupid really turns the tables on these two, and you won't want to miss a single minute of the fun!

Another wonderful writer makes her LOVESWEPT debut this month, and she fits into our lineup with grace and ease. Erica Spindler is a talented lady who has published several books for Silhouette under her own name. Her first LOVESWEPT, #423, is a charmingly fresh story called **RHYME OR REASON**. Heroine Alex Clare is a dreamer with eyes that sparkle like the crystal she wears as a talisman, and Dr. Walker Chadwick Ridgeman thinks he needs to have his head examined for being drawn to the lovely seductress. After all, he's a serious man who believes in what he can see, and Alex believes the most important things in life are those that you can't see or touch but only feel. Caught up in her sensual spell, Walker learns firsthand of the changes a magical love can bring about.

Judy Gill's next three books aren't part of a "series," but they will feature characters whose paths will cross. In **DREAM MAN, LOVESWEPT #424**, heroine Jeanie Leslie first meets Max McKenzie in her dreams. She'd conjured up the dashingly handsome hero as the answer to all her troubled sister's needs. But when he actually walks into her office one day in response to the intriguing ad she'd run, Jeanie knows without a doubt that she could never fix him up with her sister—because she wants him for herself! Max applies for the "Man Wanted" position out of curiosity, but once he sets eyes on Jeanie, he's suddenly compelled to convince

(continued)

her how right they are for each other. While previously neither would admit to wanting a permanent relationship, after they meet they can't seem to think about anything else. But it takes a brush with death to bring these two passionate lovers together forever!

Helen Mittermeyer closes the month with **FROZEN IDOL**, LOVESWEPT #425, the final book in her *Men of Ice* trilogy. If her title doesn't do it, her story will send a thrill down your spine over the romance between untouchable superstar Dolph Wakefield and smart and sexy businesswoman Bedelia Fronsby. Fate intervenes in Dolph's life when Bedelia shows up ten years after she'd vanished without a trace and left him to deal with the deepest feelings he'd ever had for a woman. Now the owner of a company that plans to finance Dolph's next film, Bedelia finds herself succumbing once again to the impossible Viking of a man whose power over her emotions has only strengthened with time. When Dolph learns the true reason she'd left him, he can't help but decide to cherish her always. Once again Helen delivers a story fans are sure to love!

In the upcoming months we will begin several unique promotions which we're certain will be hits with readers. Starting in October and continuing through January, you will be able to accumulate coupons from the backs of our books which you may redeem for special hardcover "Keepsake Editions" of LOVESWEPTs by your favorite authors. Watch for more information on how to save your coupons and where to send them.

Another innovative new feature we're planning to offer is a "900" number readers can use to reach LOVESWEPT by telephone. As soon as the line is set up, we'll let you know the number—until then, keep reading!

Sincerely,

Susann Brailey

Susann Brailey
Editor
LOVESWEPT
Bantam Books
666 Fifth Avenue
New York, NY 10103

FAN OF THE MONTH

Carollyn McCauley

After seeing the Fan of the Month in the backs of LOVESWEPTs, I wished that I'd have a chance to be one. I thought it would never happen. Due to a close friend and the people at LOVESWEPT, I got my wish granted.

I've been a reader of romance novels for twenty years, ever since I finished nursing school.

LOVESWEPTs arrive at the Waldenbooks store I go to around the first week of the month. Starting that week I haunt the store until the LOVESWEPTs are placed on the shelves, then, within two or three days, I've finished reading them and have to wait anxiously for the next month's shipment.

I have a few favorite authors: Iris Johansen, Kay Hooper, Billie Green, Sharon and Tom Curtis, and many more. As far as I'm concerned, the authors that LOVESWEPT chooses are the cream of the crop in romance. I encourage the readers of LOVESWEPT who buy books only by authors they've read before to let themselves go and take a chance on the new authors. They'll find they'll be pleasantly surprised and will never be disappointed. The books are well written, and the unusual and unique plots will capture their attention. From the first book in the line to the current ones, they have all held my attention from page one to the last, causing me to experience a variety of emotions and feelings.

Over the years of reading the different romances available, I've cut back on the amount I purchase due to the cost. LOVESWEPT has maintained such a high standard of quality that I'll always buy all six each month!

OFFICIAL RULES TO
LOVESWEPT'S
DREAM MAKER GIVEAWAY
(See entry card in center of this book)

1. NO PURCHASE NECESSARY. To enter both the
   sweepstakes and accept the risk-free trial offer, follow the
   directions published on the insert card in this book. Return
   your entry on the reply card provided. If you do not wish to
   take advantage of the risk-free trial offer, but wish to enter the
   sweepstakes, return the entry card only with the "FREE
   ENTRY" sticker attached, or send your name and address on
   a 3x5 card to : Loveswept Sweepstakes, Bantam Books,
   PO Box 985, Hicksville, NY 11802-9827.

2. To be eligible for the prizes offered, your entry must be
   received by September 17, 1990. We are not responsible for
   late, lost or misdirected mail. Winners will be selected on or
   about October 16, 1990 in a random drawing under the
   supervision of Marden Kane, Inc., an independent judging
   organization, and except for those prizes which will be
   awarded to the first 50 entrants, prizes will be awarded after
   that date. By entering this sweepstakes, each entrant accepts
   and agrees to be bound by these rules and the decision of the
   judges which shall be final and binding. This sweepstakes will
   be presented in conjunction with various book offers
   sponsored by Bantam Books under the following titles: Agatha
   Christie "Mystery Showcase", Louis L'Amour "Great American
   Getaway", Loveswept "Dreams Can Come True" and
   Loveswept "Dream Makers". Although the prize options and
   graphics of this Bantam Books sweepstakes will vary in each
   of these book offers, the value of each prize level will be
   approximately the same and prize winners will have the options
   of selecting any prize offered within the prize level won.

3. Prizes in the Loveswept "Dream Maker" sweepstakes: Grand
   Prize (1) 14 Day trip to either Hawaii, Europe or the Caribbean.
   Trip includes round trip air transportation from any major airport
   in the US and hotel accomodations (approximate retail value
   $6,000); Bonus Prize (1) $1,000 cash in addition to the trip;
   Second Prize (1) 27" Color TV (approximate retail value $900).

4. This sweepstakes is open to residents of the US, and Canada (excluding the province of Quebec), who are 18 years of age or older. Employees of Bantam Books, Bantam Doubleday Dell Publishing Group Inc., their affiliates and subsidiaries, Marden Kane Inc. and all other agencies and persons connected with conducting this sweepstakes and their immediate family members are not eligible to enter this sweepstakes. This offer is subject to all applicable laws and regulations and is void in the province of Quebec and wherever prohibited or restricted by law. In order to win a prize, residents of Canada will be required to correctly answer a time-limited arithmetical skill-testing question.

5. Winners will be notified by mail and will be required to execute an affidavit of eligibility and release which must be returned within 14 days of notification or an alternate winner will be selected. Prizes are not transferable. Trip prize must be taken within one year of notification and is subject to airline departure schedules and ticket and accommodation availability. Winner must have a valid passport. No substitution will be made for any prize except as offered. If a prize should be unavailable at sweepstakes end, sponsor reserves the right to substitute a prize of equal or greater value. Winners agree that the sponsor, its affiliates, and their agencies and employees shall not be liable for injury, loss or damage of any kind resulting from an entrant's participation in this offer or from the acceptance or use of the prizes awarded. Odds of winning are dependant upon the number of entries received. Taxes, if any, are the sole responsibility of the winners. Winner's entry and acceptance of any prize offered constitutes permission to use the winner's name, photograph or other likeness for purposes of advertising and promotion on behalf of Bantam Books and Bantam Doubleday Dell Publishing Group Inc. without additional compensation to the winner.

6. For a list of winners (available after 10/16/90), send a self addressed stamped envelope to Bantam Books Winners List, PO Box 704, Sayreville, NJ 08871.

7. The free gifts are available only to entrants who also agree to sample the Loveswept subscription program on the terms described. The sweepstakes prizes offered by affixing the "Free Entry" sticker to the Entry Form are available to all entrants, whether or not an entrant chooses to affix the "Free Books" sticker to the Entry Form.

60 Minutes to a Better, More Beautiful You!

Now it's easier than ever to awaken your sensuality, stay slim forever—even make yourself irresistible. With Bantam's bestselling subliminal audio tapes, you're only 60 minutes away from a better, more beautiful you!

__ 45004-2	**Slim Forever**	$8.95
__ 45112-X	**Awaken Your Sensuality**	$7.95
__ 45035-2	**Stop Smoking Forever**	$8.95
__ 45130-8	**Develop Your Intuition**	$7.95
__ 45022-0	**Positively Change Your Life**	$8.95
__ 45154-5	**Get What You Want**	$7.95
__ 45041-7	**Stress Free Forever**	$8.95
__ 45106-5	**Get a Good Night's Sleep**	$7.95
__ 45094-8	**Improve Your Concentration**	$7.95
__ 45172-3	**Develop A Perfect Memory**	$8.95